Charles Victor De Bonstetten

The Man of The North, and The Man of The South

Or, The Influence of Climate

SALZWASSER VERLAG

Charles Victor De Bonstetten

The Man of The North, and The Man of The South

Or, The Influence of Climate

Reprint of the original, first published in 1864.

1st Edition 2022 | ISBN: 978-3-75259-517-8

Verlag (Publisher): Salzwasser Verlag GmbH, Zeilweg 44, 60439 Frankfurt, Deutschland
Vertretungsberechtigt (Authorized to represent): E. Roepke, Zeilweg 44, 60439 Frankfurt, Deutschland
Druck (Print): Books on Demand GmbH, In de Tarpen 42, 22848 Norderstedt, Deutschland

THE MAN OF THE NORTH,

AND

THE MAN OF THE SOUTH;

OR

THE INFLUENCE OF CLIMATE.

Translated from the French of

CH-VICTOR DE BONSTETTEN.

Ce serait à tort que l'on voudrait séparer la Politique des circonstances générales de race, de climat, de configuration géographique, de traditions historiques de toute nature dont elle est à beaucoup d'égards une résultante.
BAUDRILLART.

NEW YORK

1864.

TRANSLATOR'S PREFACE.

THE author, M. de Bonstetten, whose work, *L'Homme du Midi et L'Homme du Nord*, is now given to the public in an English translation, was born in 1745 at Berne, of an ancient and noble Swiss family. Having lived eighty-seven years, he died in 1832 at Geneva. He was not without political experience, having undergone some of the sad reverses of the political treadmill. He was a friend and disciple of the celebrated Charles Bonnet, and had much intercourse and correspondence with other distinguished men of his time. Acute in his observations, cultivated in his tastes, familiar through travel with the men and the society of many climes, and casting over all the mellow hues of a highly-wrought imagination, there are few works more fascinating than the one now translated. Published thirty-seven years ago, if it has any application to our own great national crisis it will be without any party spirit, and wholly on impersonal and philosophical grounds.

Like all political prophets, M. de Bonstetten was greatly mistaken with regard to this country. The perpetuity of its unbroken unity was too dazzling to his eyes not to delude him. Any prophecy based on the institutions of a country, and not on the moral and intellectual condition of its people, is likely to be purblind. It is necessary to have a great mastery over the past and present condition of things to have much keen insight into the future. Our imagination travels much faster than our civilizing tendencies, and the real ever lags behind the ideal.

Our author attaches much importance to the modifications which climate superinduces upon our inborn faculties, and not, it would seem, without reason. But whether men are sufficiently sober in their judgments to make allowances for such things is an open question. The perusal, however, of our author's work will prove highly instructive and suggestive, and may lead to a more liberal view of the differences which exist between masses of men apparently of the same race. As there are different avenues that lead to heaven, there may be different means of arriving at political perfection. The attempt to cast everything through the same mould, to force all through the same orbit, may serve conventional purposes, but is not very descriptive of the real lines of motion peculiar to humanity. The standard of human judgment must advance with the growth of society if we would avoid the dead level of Chinese immobility.

If the work now translated will in any way aid to this end, the labor of the translator will be more than compensated.

CONTENTS.

THE

MAN OF THE NORTH

AND

THE MAN OF THE SOUTH.

Introduction.

THE TWO CLIMATES.

THE effect of climate on man has often struck me as a subject imperfectly comprehended. Climate is but one of the many causes that affect man; its influence, though always operative, is felt but gradually through effects which sometimes would appear to be foreign to it. To all the regulations made to guard against it, it occasionally yields; religious enthusiasm, attaining to a certain degree, modifies its influence; even opinions purely philosophical, like those of the Stoics, may override it. Moreover, what is North and South when the question of climate occurs? A polar altitude is but one element of climate, and a vertical altitude another. Both Greenland and Lapland may be found among the Swiss Alps, and if Northern people prized sheltered localities more, we would sometimes encounter in the North the climate of Italy. Has not the Reformation appeared here and there in Southern mountains, and do we not find despotism existing in the North?

Man's history is like a piece of tapestry on which diverse colored threads appear and disappear as they traverse the meshes of its woof. Climate is a thread of this description, appearing and disappearing at the bidding of the great disposer of all things.

In discussing facts due to a multiplicity of causes, it sometimes happens that one cause becomes isolated, which, in the nature of things, cannot act independently. Human actions never being wholly traceable to climatic agency, we must possess full knowledge of every cause affecting them before we can assign to any a special influence. Until this knowledge is obtained abstractions are pointless; it is necessary to accept life's phenomena collectively, as they present themselves to the observer's attention. Selecting the continent of Europe as a field of observation, I propose to note some of the modifications produced by climate on man in that region.

The first perceptible effect of climate on man in Europe is the feeling of renewed life, which every traveller experiences on crossing the Alps to visit the south of Europe. He is conscious of a sudden change, and, if he is watchful of his emotions, he finds himself another being according as he is on this or the other side of these grand barriers. On entering Italy its brilliant sky impresses him, its luxuriant vegetation, and the garlands of vines suspended from tree to tree above the waving grain. The colors of the landscape vary, and the mountains no longer present the same hue; the deep valleys of the Alps are gone, while naked rocks towering upwards in jagged summits seem to form a line of separation between the two skies of Italy and Switzerland. The tones of a musical and sonorous language fill the ear, accompanied with ceaseless pantomime, and a mobility of expression which excites the astonishment of the Man of the North.

The sky of the South at night is often of a deep blue, its dark mantle glittering with innumerable stars, whilst the Northern firmament is always grey, and, approaching the pole, as lifeless as the desert soil beneath it. In Italy the public worship and majestic temples, the monk's dress and gay processions, the paintings and statues, the sacred chants, the motley uniforms, the animated gesticulations of the people, everything in short through which the senses can affect a northern meditative nature, draws the spirit away from self-consciousness, leading it to act harmoniously with impressions derived from outward things.

I know not why it is one experiences among the Italians, a sentiment of personal independence never completely realized in the North! There is in Italy no annoyance from curiosity, while to the north of the Alps one is gauged, and measured according to the petty standard of every petty town he happens to pass through. In Italy people appear to be absorbed with their own impressions, to such a degree as to leave no room for intolerance, everybody acting consistently with his own proclivities. Add to this an expansion of one's nature, a development of the organs through which they operate, and a feeling of independence ensues that never dies.

Pass the Apennines on the way to Rome or Naples, and the characteristics of the South become more marked. The traveller imperceptibly enters volcanic regions; he finds the mountains, especially the rocks, assuming new shapes. Instead of sharp pinnacles peculiar to the Alps, he gazes on rounded summits, while caverns of mysterious depth, subterranean passages, and catacombs filled with the dead, open their shadowy portals before him. The lines of the distant prospect grow soft and harmonious; the boundaries of earth and sky seem to commingle; the seasons disappear in perennial verdure, and vegetation thrives with the utmost luxuriance.

The clouds of the sky of Rome display mountainous forms and aerial valleys of surpassing grandeur, and in the rosy light of sunset suggest visions of a magic land floating in space, and radiant with purple and gold. On summer nights dancing fireflies illumine the woods and fields, flashing over them by millions, concealing the earth as it were with a mantle of stars. At Naples and again in Sicily the volcano adds its magnificence to a landscape already surcharged with richness. The smoke from its colossal form rises in artificial clouds grander, more poetical, and often more terrible than the tempest-cloud; in a calm atmosphere, as it rests on the peak of the mountain, a stupendous inverted pyramid, its dark o'erhanging mass seems to threaten the earth with its downfall. Standing on Vesuvius' side during an eruption I beheld the landscape of Naples, its bay, the sea, and the islands, suddenly illuminated by the grand fiery jet of the angry crater; as the fitful flame of deep ruddy hue arose, accompanied with subterranean thunder, the sea and land beneath glowed as if overspread with a carpet of fire; profound darkness immediately followed, and the earth trembled under my feet.

To such sublime spectacles add the vestiges of former ages, the apparitions so to say of all centuries arising in every direction, and in every diverse form of ruin. It is not without emotion that on approaching these your hand rests as it were on the ages of Nero and Constantine.

Now pass the Alps from South to North. On entering Switzerland, the traveller is struck with the repose of its grand masses of mountains; their summits in the midst of the clouds appear no longer to rest on earthly foundations. Deep valleys with their mysterious recesses, and crests of mountains lost in the sky, form a solitude in which life is, as it were, suspended; water is transformed to rock, confirming the general aspect of immobility. The overhanging seas, composing the glacier region, exhibit the forms of waves, but waves without action, like all that appertains to the kingdom of death. Even the features of the people of the Alps express repose; their laws and manners denote immobility, every attempt at innovation being received with horror; moral and physical life seems to be paralysed in the realm of the glaciers.

The charm of Germany is due to its men of learning, to its taste, to a respect for talent and thought, and to a spirit of goodness and hospitality amongst the people. At Lunenbourg the aspect of the country begins to change. It is in the district of Lunenbourg that the traveller first encounters the lakes so profusely scattered over the vast surface of middle Europe. In the swampy plains their stagnant waters intensify the melancholy tone of the landscape; a lifeless expanse contracts the horizon, begetting a frightful sentiment of loneliness; it seems as if the earth had dwindled away, and was about to vanish in the dissolving mist.

In the Danish Isles, the lakes are surrounded by green hills, dotted with majestic beeches, willows, and gigantic alders, with numerous flocks and herds, and a varied cultivation, affording a pleasing prospect; but there is no sublimity or mystery, as amid the defiles and passes of the Alps. The sky of this climate, always charged with vapor, never displays the splendor of the sky of Italy.

Beyond the Baltic, the tops of the mountains have crumbled by some mysterious convulsion, and spread their débris over the immense areas around them. Rocks still stand split to their lowest foundations, the sea filling their clefts with its waters, and projecting itself far into the interior in the shape of numerous currentless rivers. In Sweden, as in Norway and in northern Russia, many of the valleys consist of lakes of still water, or otherwise form portions of the sea. The charts of Sweden and Norway represent coasts indented with lakes and deep river-like gulfs. Advancing northward we find the beech of the Baltic succeeding the fir-tree; after the firs, follow immense forests of pine decked with snow-white moss, in which the Laplanders and reindeer obtain their winter subsistence. The birch finishes the series of the great plants of the vegetable kingdom of the North, becoming almost herbaceous on the shores of the polar ocean. Here life ceases, or rather plunges into the sea where submarine pasturage supports the whale, and harbors in the dark abysses of the polar waters, a world of life unknown to man. What a spectacle to contemplate these regions of night more densely populated than the illuminated world above! The color of the polar sea proves it to be a realm of life, as a drop of water contains myriads of insects; the smallest of creation's products exists side by side with the most gigantic.

The sky of the North, obscured during half the year by clouds, is never but of a dull blue even when most beautiful; in the short nights of summer, on the Danish islands, only stars of the first magnitude are visible, placed, as it were, on a background of grey. The interval between sunset and sunrise is a moderate twilight. I remember wandering through a wood on a lovely summer night, and hearing amid the surrounding foliage the low twittering of birds perched everywhere around me; these sounds were scarcely perceptible, though harmonious with the universal repose of nature; the mild radiance of the twilight, like the music of the birds, seemed not to appeal to the senses, but rather to a mood of meditation and thought.

Although much less water falls in the North, yet, descending in fine rain and mists, it is much longer in falling than in a Southern climate. Storm-clouds and thunder-gusts are rarer, and display no majestic forms. The sky of the North possesses no striking physiognomy. The triple suns called halos are not seen as often in the North as the aurora-borealis, which again is not as frequent in Norway or in Iceland as in Greenland.

The cultivated plains of the North are divided into extensive farms, presenting everywhere high inclosures of naked walls flanked with earth and protected with trunks of trees, surrounded by deep ditches. In the centre of these vast inclosures arise square tenements projecting above the bare surface, oftentimes without trees or gardens, the wind whistling around them incessantly. Everything about the dwelling of the man of the North betokens loneliness; there is no sound but the monotonous moan of the blast; the eye rests on no object except the grass-covered tombs of ancient Scandinavians. The traveller hastens accordingly to seek comfort in the most attainable retreat. Within the great square court of the farm, sheltered from gales by its surrounding buildings, he finds every description of domestic animal with the members of the family mingled together pell-mell, presenting to view a kind of terrestrial Noah's ark.

The immense expanse of the coasts of Norway and Sweden is more violently swept by the winds than the interior of the country; these coasts, bristling with rocks and reefs, lashed by a foaming sea, and unceasingly attacked, mined, corroded as it were by the waves, appear to be a battle-ground for the raging elements. There is no sound but the dashing of breakers alternating with the wild shrieking of the wind. At the lighthouse of Kulla the atmosphere is often so dense that the lustreless sun resembles a blood-red moon, appearing gradually to yield itself to the overpowering mist. No sooner has the orb of day passed below the horizon than everywhere in the surrounding darkness the roar of wind and wave increases, raging with redoubled violence; man apparently deserted by nature abandons himself to emotions of fear. It is therefore conceivable with what delight an inhabitant of this clime retreats to his cherished dwelling, his hearthstone, his family; to that universe of enjoyment which in all ages and places the magic of the heart is so well able to provide for him.

In the foregoing sketch of the leading phenomena of the two climates I have endeavored to present points of view adapted to the ideas which I propose to develop in the body of this little work.

CHAPTER I.

AGRICULTURE.

THE direct influence of climate on man has, perhaps, been exaggerated by Montesquieu; its indirect influence, however, is extraordinary.

What contrasts we behold between the rural economy of countries in which the labors of the field are continuous, and that of countries in which the interval of labor is six, seven, and even eight months!

In the South the variety and multiplicity of crops is only limited by the labor, capital, and time which the cultivator is able to bestow on them; in the North the inhabitants give their attention only to their fields and meadows, and in high latitudes to their meadows exclusively. Before the war with the English all vegetables consumed in Norway, at Berghem and at Drontheim, were procured from Holland; it was not rare to find hay at Christiania imported from Ireland. It is only thirty or forty years ago that a now celebrated Norwegian introduced into his country the cultivation of gardens. Again in our days (1825) the vegetable market of Copenhagen is supplied by Hollanders transplanted to Denmark at the beginning of the sixteenth century, forming a little colony in the midst of a great capital, and presenting the singular spectacle of a foreign people preserving for over three centuries, the customs, language, and peculiarly quaint costume of its former estate.

A simple system of agriculture, with time to mature it, has, among the people of the North, created a spirit of order which strongly contrasts with the usages of a southern latitude. Observe how neat everything is about the dwelling of the inhabitant of German Switzerland; how clean his wells and springs, how substantial his stacks of fodder and manure, how comfortable his folds, how trim his gardens, how carefully pruned his trees; what a well garnered store of fuel and how admirable the arrangement of his domicile. This spirit of order which is noticeable on his premises he carries with him into the administration of his family, and often into the public affairs of his village. From this systematic course result those well regulated habits which constitute the basis of public security and public morality.

The cultivators and laborers of the south of Europe, never subject themselves to fixed hours. At Hyères, in the month of February, I have known washwomen to pursue their avocations all night, by the side of a stream that flowed beneath my window. At almost all seasons of the year people drive carts, and are going and coming at night, as well as during the daytime. The custom of retiring within doors, merely for slumber, prevents regular habits from taking root. It happens accordingly that the house of the man of the South is never the altar of his patriotism, whilst to the inhabitant of the North it is about the same as a shell to the snail—he could not exist without it.

In the South, through constant occupation outside their dwellings people do not concern themselves as much about their subsistence as the people of the North; from this proceeds a habit of eating little and of eating badly, since anything seems to be good to an appetite sharpened by pure air and the cravings of hunger. The kitchen of the South is often found beneath trees and under vines, or is set up in fields and in pastures. Thus do we see an onion, a bunch of grapes, a few figs, or a little garlic, suffice to sustain the Spaniard, no matter whether he is on his own soil or exposed to the risks of the battle-field.

Clothing and warmth are almost as imperative to the Northern man as subsistence. The man of the South may well dispense with these, for sunshine is often to him a substitute for heat and dress. To vanquish the inhabitant of the North it is simply necessary to obtain possession of his dwelling, whilst the man of the South can exist wherever he finds the sun, a tree, or any corner of the earth unknown to his enemy. The Spaniard, again, is an illustration of the great desideratum of the man of the South, namely, that which is due to reflection and forecast. His courage is unwisely directed; he loses through lack of reflection what experience, rationally applied, would enable him to profit by. On the other hand this very lack of reflection, coupled with the ignorance arising from it, serves the man of the South marvellously. A mind accustomed to reflection calculates danger, whilst danger to a courageous man is completely ignored. The reflecting man sees all and knows all, except the mysterious movements of the heart, and the fire of passion which often constitutes the privileged endowment of the man of the South. It is evident by what I have first stated that the southern man is disposed to act without reflecting, and the northern man to reflect without acting.

In comparing altogether the Agriculture of the North with that of the South we find the North presenting a succession of crops, that is to say, a process of cultivation in which calculations are based on the rotation system of culture; whilst in the South attention is given to a uniform mode of culture, with due regard to the quantities of anything produced in the same region.

In the South, richness of soil and a fine climate permit a greater diversity of production than in the North, where climate excludes many growths of great utility. And again, the man of the South is not only rich in various products but he has also leisure to bestow on their cultivation; the man of the North on the contrary who is confined to his dwelling during the winter months, is so destitute of time that he cannot devote much of it to labor. Most phases of national customs have their source in agriculture. It is evident that the system of agriculture in the North gives to the home-bound man leisure for thinking, and favors the growth of the imagination and ideas; whilst in the South broad sunshine and the senses in constant activity provoke thoughts out of the depths of the soul to dwell in a world of realities.

CHAPTER II.

LIBERTY.

IT is in the nature of things that political liberty, that is, the prevalence of law, should be established among nations given to order rather than among those given over to anarchy. In regions where winter prevails life requires more sanitary regulations and forethought than in the South; hence a multiplicity of laws and arrangements which a despot may not violate without imperilling his people's existence. In the North houses are necessary, clothing, fuel to give heat, and provisions to sustain life, in short, innumerable things which the ruler is obliged to conserve. It is not under an inclement and unpropitious sky that one would think of felling a tree in order to have the fruit.

Let not the forms of law be misapprehended. No constitution, apparently, is more despotic than that of Denmark, and yet no people are freer than the Danes.* The revolution rendering the king despotic, having grown out of opposition to the nobility, necessarily forced the monarch to respect the people. The principles of every monarchy require also the monarch to respect the nobles. It is, therefore, the interest of the king of Denmark to protect equally all branches of the state. Moreover the respect for things indispensable to life, peculiar to man in the North, leads to such complicated regulations, that, notwithstanding the constitutional form of despotism, a certain degree of liberty is a natural consequence. This seemed to me to be the condition of Denmark in 1799 and 1800.

False ideas prevail in the South concerning the nature of northern serfdom. When Denmark attempted to abolish serfdom the serfs themselves refused to support the measure, which shows that the institution is not so op-

---

* Danish liberty lies in the heart of a good king; but this kind of liberty lacks some guarantee for the future. In fine weather it is easy to navigate the ocean in a skiff, but who would like to expose himself for any length of time in any vessel without some guarantee against probable danger? What well-disposed king would object to sanctioning the perpetuity of a good administration!

pressive as is generally believed. The portion of the soil in Denmark abandoned to the use of a Danish peasant is so extensive that any Swiss farmer would be glad to accept it on the same conditions as those which form the tenure of the Danish serf. To give liberty to such a peasantry would be tantamount to depriving them of all sources of revenue.

Serfdom of this description was, at its origin, the most natural thing in the world. Before money came into use it was natural for the farmer to pay in labor what he could not pay for in coin; money being but the representative of labor, the latter necessarily existed before the former. It is a remark of Dalrymple in relation to this natural serfdom that history has no record of the time when slavery was abolished in England. Practically speaking, the care and anxiety of this species of reform is all on the side of the seignor, the serf alone enjoying the inappreciable happiness of freedom from responsibility. When the labor of the serf proves to be inadequate for his support the seignor is obliged to repair his dwelling and provide for his maintenance.

The evil resulting from this type of slavery evidently affects the peasant less than the lord, and still less the state. A system of serfdom greatly favors indolence and improvidence, and to such an extent that society can make no progress out of its infantile condition, but by abolishing it. Previous to the existence of industrial pursuits, social habits were so simple that actual servitude never degenerated into personal slavery. Among the Germans, says Tacitus, master and slave are on a level as to habits and education, the great difference between the serf and the freeman being this, the former remains at home while the latter goes forth to battle.

Industry once inaugurated, servitude became odious. At the origin of slavery the cultivator enjoyed a portion of his lord's estate, but when the cultivator became an artisan, or a trader, his new avocation no longer afforded him personal security, protection for his property, or the rights of justice.

The abolition of serfdom, conducted in such a way as not to injure anybody's rights, is so difficult that although Denmark has labored at this noble work for over a century she has not yet accomplished it. The gradual abolition of serfdom which we have observed in the North, whilst in the South negro slavery is seen established by those very nations which had banished servitude from their own soil proves, other circumstances being equal, that the climate of slavery is in the South and that of liberty in the North.

Let us produce a body of nations before us; let us cast our eyes over the last ten centuries of history, and we shall find that despotism becomes more and more burdensome on the shores of Africa and Asia, while liberty preponderates more and more in Europe, with shades of difference in which the easily recognised influence of climate is everywhere observable.

Great nations spring from a union of many tribes; hence the origin of all nations in freedom; the smaller a nation the more it approximated to the paternal type of government and the greater its liberty.* Traces of liberty are accordingly found in all climates; but there is

* We see a certain degree of liberty preserved in Arabia because on a desert the nature of the soil keeps man in tribal communities. On the same principle we find liberty among high mountains separating men into more or less distinct societies. It was the instinct of despotism which inspired Bonaparte with the idea of removing the great barrier of the Alps by constructing his magnificent roads over them.

this great difference between a Northern and Southern climate; in the North man's primitive liberty has been constantly perpetuated, whilst in the South it has been extinguished.

Rome possessed admirable laws, but Rome never had a fixed and stable constitution under which all classes of citizens could repose in security. The forum was ever a battle-ground for the impassioned spirits of the imperial city. How great the difference between liberty like this and the liberty of the United States of America, of England, and of old Holland, where all efforts tend to preserve the constitution which the people themselves have created. At Rome each day's labor was devoted to destroying the work of the previous day. Contrast the turbulent Grecian democracies with the democracies of Italy in the middle ages, and with the Swiss democracy! What repose characterizes the aristocracies of Zurich, Berne, Lucerne, and Soleure! What factions at Carthage, always in agitation, like all the aristocracies of Greece and Asia, as well as the aristocracies of Italy in every age.

Notwithstanding so many facts demonstrating the influence of climate, it is no less true that this influence is a cause so subordinated to other causes that the most anarchical government of all was that of Iceland, while Sparta and Venice underwent but few revolutions. The liberty of man is in the ascendency of his reason, the liberty of a nation is in that of its law, which is nothing but reason applied to the body politic. There is no development of either except though a knowledge universally diffused of the relationships by which good laws are maintained among nations and sound morality among individuals. To develop the growth of reason should be the aim of all governments, for with that growth liberty exists everywhere, and without it nowhere.

A representative constitution for nations without enlightenment does not insure liberty, whilst a constitution without national representation secures freedom so long as principles can be universally diffused and provision made for their discussion.

CHAPTER III.

INDIFFERENCE TO THE FUTURE.

INDIFFERENCE to the future is a remarkable trait in Southern character. At Rome and at Naples, indeed throughout Italy, it is customary to consume the whole of the day's provision, so that in the best households, and in many inns, there is not a crust of bread in the evening, and frequently not a crumb to be had. Whatever remains of the day's supply is appropriated by the Italian domestics, who regard a surplus as their property. If strangers prudently provide beforehand, by making purchases in times of plenty, the prodigality of servants is such as to render their care a loss. When servants do not, by some miracle, expend their wages in advance they will, on receiving them, if women, invest them in trinkets, and if men, in silver buckles or entertainment at a cabaret. On my representing to these people the inconvenience of having no reserve fund for accidents, they gravely inquired of me where they could conceal money, considering it to be the perquisite of robbers as were their masters' stores for themselves.

Let the reader reflect a moment on the influence of a climate producing a harvest almost every month of the year. It is evident that precaution could not be generated in such a climate! At Hyères the orange trees would be laden with fruit the whole winter were it not gathered for exportation before it reaches maturity; the gardens bloom throughout the year; olives are gathered in winter; the sea is almost always accessible, and birds are so abundant as to supply both the poor and the rich. Honey might be consumed at all times, as the bees are constantly busy. In Provence snails abound, and are prized by all gourmands. Let us add that in the South the sun and the labors of the field are substitutes for clothing and fuel. I have seen an old man at Hyères sitting all winter in the sun, amusing himself singing the Latin terms of the service which he had caught in his attendance at mass.

Oppose to this picture the terrible phenomenon of winter in high latitudes where death seems to descend with the snowflakes. Imagine man buried alive in this vast tomb of nature; fancy the long winter nights and blasting frosts that accompany them! Preceding this universal lifelessness comes the falling leaf, admonishing man of his mortality. The beneficent streams and fountains are stayed in their course; the tempest is loosened in its fury; cultivation ceases long before the approach of winter; the birds migrate, and all signs of life go with them; in the desolate forests bears and wolves alone remain their sole inhabitants. The sea is inaccessible, and everything betokens famine. The necessities of life and the means of providing for them are as far apart as if separated by an immense abyss. Abandoned thus by nature it is no wonder that man strains every nerve to anticipate his future wants.

There is accordingly for the man of the North a season consecrated to forethought and reflection; while in the South man has no urgent necessity to interfere with or arrest the play of his imagination. In this respect there is an immense difference between the man of the North and the man of the South!

The necessities of life in the North strongly stimulate the thinking faculties and develop habits of reflection. For self-protection in winter, man constructs houses and procures supplies of food; a season of dearth brings economy and provident calculation. In the South, on the contrary, man lives from day to day; crop follows crop scarcely requiring a thought; foliage and flowers display unfading luxuriance; the present is everything, the future being lost sight of in a ceaseless activity of the imagination and unbounded enjoyment. Worship in the South is always dramatic and entertaining; miracles transpire daily; whilst in the North religion confines itself to the future, drawing on the past for its lessons and solely preaching to man the empire of reason over the passions.

Improvidence produces indolence, which, in a climate where the fibres of sensibility are always active, and the mind always interested, gives perpetual delight; whilst this same indolence weighs down a Northern nature insensible to that intestine vitality which imagination alone can generate. An Italian woman will remain at her window unwearied during the entire day, simply glancing at men passing as they happen to strike her fancy or not, whilst a Northern woman would die of ennui.

CHAPTER IV.

RELIGION.

ON comparing the religion of Northern with that of Southern people we find a less climatic difference than in their phases of political liberty.

The various sects of the reformed religion that have originated in the North have never sustained themselves in the South. It is because imagination adds to faith, while it is the nature of reason to abstract from faith whatever is not doctrinal. Sects born in the North are, like all mystic sects, the result of a sentiment generated in retirement and obscurity, and always introverted; whilst the religions of the South, born under the bright rays of the sun, tend to the adoration of external objects. Mystics proceed from the heart to the object; Southern nations on the contrary proceed from the object to the heart. It follows accordingly that worship in the South directs itself to whatever affects the senses, and in the North to whatever disposes one to contemplation. Mystics love to fill the chambers of the soul with visions, as Italians love to decorate the walls of their temples with paintings. What obstacles Moses had to contend with in preventing the worship of idols among the Jews! During the Lower Empire the worship of the senses in the South triumphed over the Iconoclasts, whilst in the North it is now abolished.

Christianity at its origin held to mysticism; it was simply a worship of the heart combined with a love of our fellow-creatures, particularly of the oppressed and suffering. It is owing to this that the reformers did not pretend to be innovators. They did nothing in fact but lop from religion the parasite branches which a Southern sun had grafted on it. It was a development of reason that led to a reform, through a protest against abuses. If the human mind should ever again retrograde, it will probably retreat upon the domain of the imagination and adopt leading dogmas which, owing to advances made by reason, are now repudiated.

CHAPTER V.

OPINIONS, FASHIONS, CUSTOMS, COTERIES.

IN countries where the passions rule, the opinion of a coterie, and of society, is nearly powerless; every man being occupied with his own thoughts has no time to bestow on the opinions of others. Hence it is that in a country like Italy, the opinion of a coterie has the least weight, whilst among nations of social habits opinion is the god to which all render homage.

There is nothing more remarkable than the invariability of the laws, of the religious usages and customs which, according to Montesquieu, prevails in the Orient. This invariability amongst Eastern people is accounted for by the great influence which a wholly sensuous religion exercises over them. The more a religion affiliates with the senses the greater the number and variety of ceremonial observances. In countries where reason rules and not the senses, religious observances are all but null, or at least, arbitrary; where imagination rules they are woven into the tissue of daily life, and are perpetuated by the clergy who have an interest in maintaining whatever gives them dominion over their fellow-men.

The people of the South stand in such need of fixed customs that those who do not abound in religious observances, as, for example, the Chinese, draw themselves together by civil practices, in assuming ceremonial codes as complicated as the religious codes of the ancient Egyptians. It is by comparing the religious practices of the South with those of the North that the great difference between the two climates becomes so striking. Tacitus remarks that the ancient Germans, instead of possessing temples and statues, had consecrated forests where the gods revealed themselves through the reverential spirit which these sacred groves inspired. *Deorumque nominibus appellant secretum illud quod solâ reverentiâ vident.* In the churches of the North of Europe an affectation of nudity prevails, as in the ceremonies of Northern mystics, an absence of positive form, to such an extent that these holy men scarcely dare to move, whilst the Southern dervish will whirl myriads of times on the point of his foot without stopping.

The religious faith of all nations is, as we have seen, ever controlled by some dominant sentiment. Among all people superstition is born of fear. The oriental Ahriman and Ormuzd, the two geniuses respectively of good and evil, arose out of the sentiments of fear and of hope. Faith rests upon sentiment even among civilized nations. Did not incredulity at the English court succeed to the terror inspired by puritanism? The impiety of the Regency, was it not born out of the ennui produced by the asceticism of the aged Louis Quatorze? And do we not in our own day see all attempts in France to revive religious motives characterized by great sensitiveness to the impiety of the Revolution?

The great principle of the immutability of customs and usages is due to religion. A monk's garb is simply the dress of antiquity preserved by custom, and in the course of time consecrated by religious statute. So ancient are the forms of religious exercises that many of those used in the mass are said to have been practised by the Romans before the advent of Christianity, for example, the manner of raising the hands in prayer. *Palmas ad sidera tendens* is no longer employed except in the service of the mass.

How slight the connexion is between religion and the superstitious faith of Southern people appears in the circumstance of a gentleman of my acquaintance at Naples, who had some pretension to intellect, denying the existence of a deity, and at the same time believing in the miracles of St. Januarius!

The money-making spirit which prevails amongst the most enlightened people of Europe tends to favor manufactures, and to vary gradually everything belonging to fashions and customs. The mutability of luxury singularly counterbalances the immutability which religion is constantly tending to establish amongst men.

Ancient Egypt was formerly the centre of every religious usage, of every unalterable custom, and of every form of morals which religion could establish amongst men. We find in our days the same immobility in the Indian peninsula. Modern France, on the contrary, is the centre of change in all those matters, presenting a singular contrast to the immutable customs of the Orient. In France, nothing is permanent but changes of fashion and diverse modes of display. Fashion being simply a love of elegance among the superior classes naturally changes rapidly in order not to become vulgarized by imitations of the inferior classes. Hence a source of inconstancy which often sweeps away customs, principles, distinctions, everything that reason strives to fix as unalterable.

France situated between the glowing sky of the South and the dreamy regions of the North seems to present a happy fusion of the two ways of living in these two climates. In countries where the passions predominate, man is accessible only through the passions; in those where thought prevails, only through thought. It is necessary to *prove* to the Northern man what you are obliged to make the Southern man *feel*. The Frenchman alone is at once accessible through the two avenues of reason and sentiment. We find his mind accordingly more open to all kinds of truth than that of any other nationality; he may be susceptible to prejudice, but, not being rooted, his prejudice will be less dangerous than that of the man of routine, or of him who is under the dominion of passion. Toleration is a natural consequence of this trait, for toleration cannot exist among men who never abjure an opinion nor among those whom the passions sway and who are obedient to the dictation of priests. This same temper of soul, equally open to influences of the head or heart, prevents the French from being profound when no great object keeps them bound to an idea, so that, in France, the same man may be superficial in his opinions and yet become profound in his researches.

A nation always prone to influences, whether of the head or heart, will be volatile in its tastes but not inconstant in things demanding constancy, since the sensibility which breeds preferences perpetuates them less through habit than through taste constantly kept in a state of excitement. Such a nation is eminently social because, accessible through the head as through the heart, it has more to gain by intercourse with mankind than any other nation. It will also be remarkable for geniality, since it alone possesses that tact which implies that man is at once capable of thinking and feeling, which dreamy or impulsive natures can never comprehend. It will be carried away by novelty since nothing will prevent it from constantly indulging it.

When a little variety happens to be associated with a taste for novelty there ensues a love of fashion which consists much less in a desire to possess any particular object than in a ceaseless longing after variety; a thing is coveted less for itself than as a substitute for what it replaces. The taste of such a nation will be perfect in ephemeral matters, and often mediocre in appreciating things dependent on profound sentiment. Accustomed to feel and think simultaneously it will treat much on matters of taste, and will badly appreciate what can be but felt or thought. Its politeness will supersede its principles, whilst the more northern nations have more principles than politeness. A nation naturally good soon forgets injuries, its benevolent sentiments always affording an open door to easy and speedy reconciliation.

A nation more volatile than reflective is incapable of being governed by a constant love of an unwieldy constitution; it prefers monarchy, because to fixed and just principles monarchy often superadds a variety of forms; national goodness combined with a lively sense of justice and order leads such a nation to reject a blind and brutal despotism almost as naturally as its volatility leads it to repudiate a spirit of republicanism.

There is in the theory of moral sentiments a phenomenon which, perhaps, has not yet been developed. In every class composed of like individuals, for instance, what is called a coterie, a central opinion is formed which gradually controls the entire body. As there is a peculiar pleasure in cherishing sentiments in harmony with those of people with whom we associate, it follows that in exclusive communities a dominant sentiment prevails. A person may without any trouble differ in ideas from those associated with him, but not in conventional opinions.

An opinion which is formed from the union of accordant opinions is very noticeable in political bodies, as, for example, in aristocratic senates. In these constituted and sovereign bodies are formed maxims which when once established in fixed laws no longer admit of discussion. Like the ballast of a ship they keep the great political machine in order, and are valuable as long as the relationships on which they are based, continue; when these terminate they lead to political death.

In reunions destined merely for amusement every individual is judged according to the standard opinion established in the coterie he belongs to. It is not unusual to see persons of merit become victims of conventional opinion where mediocrity prevails. The more cohesive and exclusive a society is, and the more its character, good or bad, is developed, the more despotic and proscriptive it becomes.

The spirit of party once fixed in an exclusive society it becomes impossible to cross its limits, seeing that whoever would free himself from it would be as one against many. But it must be observed, that opinions being once confined in a uniform circle, it is to be seen that in this prison the strongest sentiments are swallowed up by the weakest, so that party spirit tends to concentrate itself and to become more and more restricted; all discussion, being gradually given up in leading ideas, at length becomes null. Hence the prejudices of small towns, which are nothing but expanded coteries wherein every ray of knowledge is extinguished if it is not constantly renewed by study.

The less an opinion is discussed the more widely it is received, for it is discussion, it is knowledge which circumscribes opinion. The prodigious sway which dogma exercises over ignorant minds is thus accounted for. A ruling opinion no longer discussed is soon hedged round with conclusions and insignificant opinions which at length overpower the mind and ultimately exclude from it the faintest rays of intelligence.

What I state of coteries applies to every assemblage of men great or small. Political bodies of every kind have their maxims; every nation has its national opinion, its own peculiar characteristic; each town, each village possesses its own creed, its own dogma. But the sciences, commerce, the fashions, and the varied march of time and events constantly break down those barriers which tend to isolate man from man and to narrow more and more the circle of their stagnant conceptions.

CHAPTER VI.

MENDICITY.

I REGARD mendicity as ineradicable in the South. There the impulse of pity is a standard need which propagates mendicity quite as much as lack of employment. There is no spectacle more remarkable than Rome on fête days, when the people display their picturesque finery, and the beggars their exaggerated costumes in the shape of the most *recherché* rags, in other words, the most disgusting ones, contriving to expose counterfeit wounds, limbs, and sores, and oftentimes simulating the last stages of death. A religion based on martyrdom is always fostering the sentiment of pity; on grand fête-days and on penitential occasions it is as much a necessity for the devout to give as for a beggar to receive. At the North mendicity can be regulated by the police and by poorhouse laws, which is an impossibility in the South.

CHAPTER VII.

HABIT.

THE spirit of order and the love of law characterizing the people of the North beget habits oftentimes of an imperious nature. To be constantly the slave of habit unwings imagination and deadens the spirit. I am aware that the man of letters loves regularity in material life; but he loves it only because it enables him to forget this material life and to surrender himself to active and refreshing thought. Except a few rare instances of men who control their own destiny in spite of habit, a majority of mediocre minds pass through life in monotonous slumber, awakening only when some unforeseen circumstance arouses them. In the South variety of productions, diversity of labor rising therefrom, the habit of sleeping, of working, and of eating at all hours, the fact of not being housed, of not being coupled with all that surrounds us; divine worship, processions, religious associations which are but a series of fêtes and spectacles; the habit of being engrossed by love at all periods of life, all these aid, in the South, in expanding the imagination.

Habit is one of heaven's great gifts, since, in the course of time, it alone extinguishes all sorrow. We become attached to our habits as we advance in life through a kind of friendly instinct. It is the opiate of habit which enables us to descend to the grave so gently and imperceptibly as not to be sensible of our approach to it. *Subrepit non intellecta senectus.* But when it concerns us to live, and not to die, nothing is more destructive than habit, for it robs us daily of some of life's consciousness, converting us into mere moving shadows, incapable either of loving, feeling, or thinking.

When we travel, that is, when we cast off our habits, time seems to expand for our benefit, thus indicating that a flood of new sensations has overwhelmed us and checked the empire of habit. On the other hand, in a uniform state of happiness life fades away as if lost in a thickening mist; we become insensible to its joys, through the absence of everything to provoke its vigor. I have often admired the repose of men of fifty and sixty years vegetating hour after hour in cafés and other familiar resorts, without conversation and without thought, solely occupied day after day completing the circle of their habits.

CHAPTER VIII.

POESY.

THE poets of Germany, Denmark, Sweden, and England love to dwell on the beauties of nature, especially landscape. They devote themselves to this much more than the poets of the South. The reason of this is that, in the North, long winters produce a yearning for spring, or rather summer, there being, as Tacitus remarks, no spring or autumn in northern regions.

In countries of perennial bloom the seasons imperceptibly dissolve into each other; never do we find in Southern regions those terrible contrasts which, even when compared with the summer charms of Lapland, a Northern winter presents. De Buch gives a glowing picture of a fine morning at Altegor, the most northerly settlement in Lapland. "The weather," he says, "was mild, the sky serene; and the sea being calm and dazzling, was disturbed only by the gambols of numerous whales whose movements resembled sudden tempests. The widespread verdure of the coasts, the attractiveness of the forests, and the innumerable flocks that enlivened the landscape, all this was delightful." Delightful indeed, *transeuntibus* the inhabitants might exclaim, to all who, like him, were temporary visitors. Only because these pictures are rare do they excite strong and ineffaceable emotions. Homer, Ossian, and Milton, have perhaps been leading poets only because, being deprived of sight, the memory of what they had seen was embellished by their regrets at no longer appreciating those emotions whereof the habit, if they had not been blind, would have robbed them in the long run.

* * * *

One might be tempted to believe that in a Southern climate there was more of poesy in people's breasts than is found under the glacial skies of the North. History however seems to demonstrate the contrary.

Poesy supposes two things; sentiment to give it birth called inspiration, and language adapted to the expression of this sentiment. With the man of the North sentiment is more concentrated than with the man of the South, and on this account, always nearer inspiration. Under a Southern sky sentiment, in being confined to exterior objects, evaporates in enjoyment; under the dun sky of a Northern climate it is self-concentrated. The result of this is that the feeling of the man of the North is deeper than that of the man of the South who, owing (as a compensation) to the pliability of organs, possesses sooner a harmonious language.

Nothing is less known, even in this inquisitive century, than the customs, the language, and the poetry of the Scandinavians previous to the introduction of Christianity.* The religion, customs, language, and even history of these semi-barbarous people consists entirely of poetry, miracle, heroism, atrocious crime or great virtue. The history of man is so confounded with that of gods, demons, sylphs, and gnomes, the reality is so exaggerated by the marvellous, that a picture of this people seems like a drama in which fabulous giants perform amid the sombre shadows and mysterious clouds of a tempest. The narrations of the mighty deeds of the Icelandic Sagas are half prose and half verse. But all this poetic

---

* Towards the year 1000 A.D.

panorama is, unfortunately, poetry in the rudest form of expression; objects appear as if seen through a mist, the mind being allowed to conjecture more than the poetic rendering conveys. In reading these Sagas, these poetic sketches, containing so many treasures unknown to the concatenated poetry of civilized people, one is frequently tempted to complete them. It is not because the polar nations were wanting in a sentiment for beauty. In the twelfth century, in the time of Saxo-Grammaticus and Snorro Sturleson, no man in Europe wrote Latin with more skill and purity than these distinguished historians.

The advent of Christianity at the North, and the introduction of a foreign and scientific language (Latin) which immediately followed, served to arrest the progress of these poetically barbarous people in perfecting their national tongue.

After the destruction of paganism these poetic visions, to be found only in the narratives of the Scalds, only in the Icelandic sagas, slowly and steadily disappeared. On the revival of a taste for the national idiom, after a second barbaric period of four or five centuries, nothing but a rude language existed which it required a long time to perfect, not according to national character, but in accordance with a foreign model. The result of all this is, that, through the retarded development of the national idiom a higher order of poetry amongst northern nations declared its birthright.

The relationship of words to thought is so intimate and so delicate that every thought necessarily leaves its trace in language, so that the language we use is but the result of what has existed for ages before us. But this series of impressions, this thread on which thought is sustained in language, breaks whenever the native idiom is supplanted by a foreign tongue. The native language preserves the charm of association; it is eminently the language of the heart, of the season of youth, and consequently of poesy.

The difference between the languages of the northern and southern portions of the continent of Europe is this: the Swedish, Danish, and German languages, have never been essentially modified by conquests, while the languages of the civilized people of the South have always been affected, or in other words, mutilated by those of their conquerors.

The development of thought among the Germans has been modified, if not retarded by their imitation of foreign models; their language, however, has remained intact, whilst the people of the South have repeatedly lost theirs. Hence the Germanic dialects harmonize more closely with the national character than the composite language of the South, a large portion of the terms of which have neither root nor correlative. To these drawbacks add that the historic memories of the always enslaved people of the South can have no such ennobling incentives as the all but ever victorious and heroic people of the North. I conclude from all this that the languages of the South composed of dead languages* have, for the people who speak them, reached their final stage of development, whilst the languages of the North, grafted on living roots, have additional developments in store for them.

The ancient Hellenic tongue is the only one that unites to the advantages which climate gives to sentiment and thought the good fortune of never having been affected by foreign idioms.

---

* Iberian, Celtic, Latin, Greek, Gothic, etc.

CHAPTER IX.

SUICIDE.

MONTESQUIEU was justified in stating that Northern people commit suicide without adequate motives, whilst Southern people, in depriving themselves of life, know why they do so. Suicide thus shows itself to be a disease among Northerly nations, while in the South it is an explosion of violent passion, the object of which is rather to destroy the author of one's trouble than to use the dagger against oneself.

I heard in Copenhagen that the suicides in the kingdom of Denmark numbered over one hundred and twenty per annum. When I was in that city it was customary for every one committing suicide to cast himself out of a window, so contagious is example in this malady. I have never been able to verify a single case of suicide during my travels in Italy, although I doubt not many occur. There is in the South an exuberance of life, an emotional need which keeps every organ in perpetual excitement; there is a constant disposition to enjoy impressions obtained through outward things, like the bird which all sounds, all objects, and all motions animate.

I shall never forget dining one day with a young Englishman of a charming figure, rich, and very high in rank, who begged me to remain after his guests withdrew as he had a secret to confide to me. The secret he wished to disclose consisted of an ennui such as to lead him to think of taking his own life. I was then quite young, and felt deeply impressed by the contrast which his good fortune and weariness of life presented; I blessed heaven and my father for having endowed me with a taste for study, a love of life and of labor.

The habit of merging sensation into self-consciousness, admirable when for purposes of reflection, becomes injurious, when it is not accompanied with great intellectual activity. I have known mediocre men become almost imbecile through the study of German metaphysics. The habit of detaching oneself from outward impressions seems to paralyse the organs; the enjoyment of pleasant sentiments is lost, while the sorrows and trials, inseparably connected with life, assume additional force. Freedom from want, always forestalled amongst the rich, gradually extinguishes pleasant impulses in order to consign man to grief alone. Ennui, which is but a trifling incident when transient, becomes destructive when it is prolonged. It is easy to travel a quarter of a league on a desert, but placed on the sands of Arabia unable to find one's way, is an image of him who becomes a helpless victim to ennui. The man of the South is a stranger to all this, whilst nothing is more common on this side of the Alps, particularly in the North, where long winters give to the mind the habit of detaching itself from outward impressions, and of turning inwardly on itself. Is not an empty mind feeding upon itself, the same as being condemned to languish on a desert?

CHAPTER X.

DRUNKENNESS.

DRUNKENNESS, much more common in the North than in the South, is in the former a selfish indulgence which seems to increase the higher the degree of latitude. Brandy is the poison of Norway, Lapland, and of all people dwelling beyond the Baltic. Among these people drunkenness is regarded as a sign of wealth, as a badge of distinction which, however disgraceful, seems to flatter their vanity. "I have something to drink," is a common saying of the rich Norwegians over their cups. To hear the Danes one would suppose that without brandy there was no such thing as health or medicine. With the man of the South wine is an ordinary beverage, which he never abuses because it is habitual with him; whilst the man of the North cherishes it as a deceitful mistress which leads him to ruin. Now that destitution (1810) often deprives the

Southern man of the wine he is accustomed to have on his table drunkenness is reviving, there being many fathers of families who waste their wages at a cabaret rather than share them with others.

CHAPTER XI.

INSTRUCTION.

WITH very little instruction a Southern man makes much more rapid progress in the sciences than a Northern man. But in order to effect this progress it is found extremely difficult to fix the imagination on the objects of instruction. In the South all the faculties are so active, there is such a tendency to breed ideas and arouse emotions, that it is hard to discover the precise moment of settling a new principle in a young scholar's bráin. The mind, like the soil—and to a much greater extent—is so prolific, that the more decided the natural talent the more do the flowers and parasites already rooted obstruct the teacher's efforts. Once, however, the seeds of science are planted, there follows a rapid and vigorous growth.

In the North the mind inclines more readily to reflection than in the South; and the tendency to subjectivity is much more natural to it. But in frosty latitudes the mind has not, as in the South, that vigorous energy which springs at once to the highest reach of thought. In the North, method, time, and persistent effort are essential in order to supply the deficiencies of nature. Comparatively speaking, however, the mental productions of the two climates are equal. The man of the South strives to discard superfluous ideas, while the object of the man of the North is firmly to develop an idea. In the South thought must be constantly pruned, whereas in the North it must be elaborated by laborious repetition.

It is understood that it is of the sciences that I speak, for, in the Fine Arts, all equality ceases. The tropics claim so justly all that belongs to beauty that the artists of the North have at all times felt the necessity of a change of climate; all those who have distinguished themselves as artists owe their cultivation to Italy, or at least have felt instinctively the necessity of living there. When we shall have been taught to distinguish better than we do now the faculty of thinking from that of feeling it will be seen how important it is for the artist to live in a land where the imagination is paramount.

In France the Fine Arts are, if I may use the expression, much better reasoned on than felt, while in Italy they are much better felt than reasoned on. At Paris one is almost forced into compliance with the taste of the day; one is harassed by discussions about that which can only be felt. All this is an obstacle to the growth of genius which, in order to mature itself, requires repose and retirement, like the diamond whose crystallization is deranged by the slightest movement.

Contemplate the privileged life of an artist at Rome! His studio is so secluded that we might almost regard him as an anchorite. The windows shut out the ground, permitting the sky only to be visible, ever clear and serene except when varied by luminous clouds or the dark canopy of a passing shower. The Apollo Belvidere, the Laocöon, the Venus de' Medici, are the sole forms which fix his attention; a few favorite poets are his sole study. The century he lives in is almost unknown to him. *Quid Iridatem terreat unicè securus.* When he leaves his studio, it is to wander amid the ruins of ancient Rome, in company with cherished phantoms with which alone he loves to linger. Does he crave diversion he betakes himself to some temple consecrated to the saint of the day, and in a magnificent structure, in the presence of the loveliest women, listens to the music of angels.* Does he long to enter an assembly of the Olympic gods he resorts to an inviting gallery where the masterpieces of centuries await his presence. The indifference of the holy city to all things of a gossiping character is such that, notwithstanding one is in the midst of a great capital, he is more independent than if alone on the barren wastes of Sahara. The poor may live in Rome without shame. An artist of my acquaintance visited Rome with thirty crowns in his pocket, and supported himself for three years in some way unknown to myself. On returning to his native land he acquired a fortune. Mentioning the circumstance to me he exclaimed: "I am ashamed of it, for my talent is disappearing in the execution of insignificant works. Were I not married I would immediately betake myself to Rome and again enjoy the solitude and poverty of my younger days." Walking one

* There was formerly a fête almost every day in the year in honor of some Saint in some one of the 360 churches in Rome, at which there was music and assemblages of the most beautiful women.

day on the heights of Aqua Pauli in company with an artist about to leave Rome I saw the tears spring to his eyes on contemplating the city from which he was so soon to depart.

At Paris an artist passes his life away listening to discussions on art, while at Rome he lives only to see and to feel. At Paris ambition exhausts talent in subjecting it to the caprices of false connoisseurs; at Rome an artist's ambition consists only in surpassing himself. Talent and feeling are interdependent, the purer the one the more perfect the other, talent becoming corrupt when grafted upon alien sentiment.

In fostering the Fine Arts all that is necessary is to remove obstacles. Obstacles, however, often prevail even against the power of kings. A cloudy sky, a certain degree of temperature, the nature of the people with whom we are compelled to live, are all obstacles of an insurmountable character. What is necessary to the artist is simply the privilege of seeing and feeling the beautiful, of entertaining noble ideas, and of indulging in all diversions that minister to his talent, and this is precisely what Rome formerly provided for him and what perhaps he may even yet at the present day enjoy there.

CHAPTER XII.

LITERATURE AND CRITICISM.

IT is surprising to find among the works of erudition and criticism of the South a greater number of a mediocre character than can be found among those of the North. The Italians, for example, have issued innumerable volumes treating of the remains of antiquity on their soil, and yet without throwing much new light on the subject.* With a few faint glimpses and numerous citations the antiquaries of Italy produce long dissertations which never amount to anything. Facility of execution in the south of Europe leads to the production of mediocre works. Too great facility in speaking and writing is indeed a shoal on which the lively imaginations of all climates

* When this was written I had no knowledge of the writings of Visconti, who is the first antiquary of genius in Italy. It is the misfortune of mediocre writers at the South to drown their thoughts in words.

are wrecked; the more numerous ideas are, the more culture is necessary to give them value. On returning from the south of France I noticed at Avignon a cluster of neglected windmills, their wings still in motion but turning to empty hoppers. Here, I said to myself, is an image of Southern intellect when severe culture makes no amends for defects born of its richness and vivacity. Erudites prone to publish are like these mills that move but grind nothing. With a store of ill-digested facts, and an uncommon facility in the marshalling of words and ideas, many produce indifferent works that, with greater labor, would compose good ones.

Less activity of the imagination, and greater habit of reflection, secures greater solidity to the works of Northern erudites. The danger with them is relying too much on systems; the same inertness which induces an Italian to write without thinking induces a German to cling to one idea which he believes to be general, and the Frenchman to adhere to the opinion of the day.

There is one mode of literary activity the Italians do not possess, and that is newspapers. Facility in this line is a great danger for restless and impatient minds.

The judgment of the man of the North is generally better than that of the man of the South. But if this superiority of judgment belongs only to the want of imagination, it will have too little scope. When such persons pass out of the narrow circle of their own ideas, no absurdity is too great for them. How many men reputed of sound judgment have committed grave errors in times of excitement by overstepping the confines of daily experience!*

Good criticism is evidently a fruit that ripens much faster in the North than in the South. But when Southern nations bestow on their talents the careful culture which they require, we see them possess Quintilians and Longinuses which the men of the North have not yet equalled.

Mental culture not only tends to augment the number and richness of our ideas, but to perfect the instrumentality of thought itself. In a partial and chance development of our facul-

* The French Revolution illustrates this remark. How many instances of excellent magistrates showing incapacity in political affairs the moment they presumed to step outside the circle of their daily duties! Similar results are visible in armies where mere men of system are so frequently beaten by intelligent men without it.

ties, many defects both of mind and character ensue. It is only by exercising our faculties steadily, methodically, and conjointly, that they become of mutual benefit.

A harmonious development of all our faculties, apparently serving the intellect alone, contributes still more towards producing that repose of the heart which constitutes happiness. An undisciplined imagination wearies and misleads the man it agitates. A mental turmoil too continuous hardens and exhausts the mind, rendering it sterile and incapable of cherishing any desire for happiness.

The forces of nature in every direction seem gradually tending towards unity and harmony. All partial development is, consequently, antagonistic to order. A complete culture of the mind, with that of the heart to correspond, has produced the grand imposing characters which stand out on the pages of history. The man of superior intelligence will accordingly become the social type; he also symbolizes the happiest man, for the virtues which seem to exist for the benefit of others, provide also for the happiness of him who possesses them, as our vices, apparently acting externally, ever react in some shape and wound ourselves.

Men of every clime need to ponder over these truths, active minds in order to excite self-distrust, and less active in order to rest their hopes on labor, method, and courage, which alone form the true foundation of self-dependence.

CHAPTER XIII.

SUSCEPTIBILITY.

THE inhabitants of the North confine themselves to their dwellings one third of the year, deprived of all resources but those which they find in their families. Hence the somewhat too meditative character of the Germans; hence their taste for metaphysics, mysticism, and the speculative sciences; hence their gentle and affectionate attachment to those who know how to comprehend and appreciate them. Uniform habits, limited knowledge of the world, and but little friction with society, joined to respect for rank and law, render the Germans formalists, and give them defects characteristic of all German races. Their susceptibility takes umbrage at whatever is not accordant with their prescribed forms and usages.

Susceptibility is a weakness of character little known in France, and still less in Italy.

Passionate natures like those of the Italians, are irritable but not susceptible; a predominant feeling is too much taken up with itself to have any link of connexion with that of others. The gaiety of the French, their great sociability and their self-esteem free them from this defect; the English escape it sometimes through the characteristic quality of their race, pride.* The Germans, less passionate than the Italians, less proud than the English, less social than the French, are eminently susceptible. If they fail to seize at once the import of a word, or the point of a jest, they turn it over in their minds, subjecting it to the ordeal of reflection. Now, to isolate a word or phrase which owes its value to inspiration or to juxtaposition with other

* There is an important exception to this in the large class of English females occupying an inferior position in their own country, who, in foreign lands, exhibit susceptibility in a very foolish, pretentious manner. Instead of regarding people with whom they happen to be thrown in contact in society, as socially qualified for their company, they view them, if not specially introduced to them, as exceptional characters and unworthy of attention. This class of English women exhibit their susceptibility still more ludicrously to their compatriots, treating them disdainfully as if of inferior rank, being wholly ignorant that the superior classes in England are most conspicuous for politeness and affability.

words is to change its nature entirely. Born of a passing sentiment its meaning is not to be judged at the bar of reflection, where it would not be understood, seeing that sentiment cannot be translated into thought. We may *reason* on the outward relations of impressions and sentiments, but we can appreciate their real value only in experiencing them.

The susceptibility of the Germans is noted in the proverbial expression of *querelle d'Allemand.* In France no idea can be formed as to how social life may be disturbed by the susceptibility which renders all gaiety perilous. This defect is very rare in large cities.

To be influenced by some leading feeling is the counterpoise to this susceptibility. I have never contemplated the sublime constancy of the Roman deputies sent to Tarentum as recorded by Tacitus without admiration; grossly insulted by a fickle and barbarous people, they nevertheless appeared in the theatre before the assembled multitude and acquitted themselves of their mission, disdaining to make any allusion to the indignities heaped upon them as they passed through the streets.

In German towns, especially where a *patois* is spoken—that is, an imperfect dialect which has never been written—any indulgence of wit or humor is impossible. And as pleasantry is often the expression of a cheerful heart, this refined gaiety can never exist amongst men who neither know what they say nor what they hear.

Susceptibility is one of the causes of that gossiping taste which distracts small towns, in which pretensions are as incomprehensible as the meaning of words. In a small town where, through ignorance of its own language, people never very justly know what is said, and what others feel, the shock of self-love amongst them is like that of drunken men confined in the cell of a prison-house.

CHAPTER XIV.

A DIGRESSION ON PATOIS.

THE reader will allow me to make a digression on the disadvantage of neglecting the study of cultivated languages. It is very unfortunate that the German portion of Switzerland, which requires but little to possess a pure language, should be precisely that wherein a defective language prevails. French Switzerland began to discard its patois nearly a hundred years ago. I am at a loss to know how it is that Italian Switzerland, much less cultivated perhaps at that time than German Switzerland, should have had a better language than the neighboring districts of Piedmont and Milan.

The jargon heard daily in some of the German towns of Switzerland contains expressions so coarse that I have seen the amiable poet Matheson blush on hearing them fall from very modest lips. The accent of the most enlightened town of German Switzerland, Zurich, is so harsh and discordant, the ear of the stranger is so wounded by it, that one is slow in discovering that these sounds convey ideas, and oftentimes ideas of a high order.

Foreigners will scarcely comprehend that in a majority of the towns of German Switzerland there are really three languages in vogue, the French, the German of the peasantry blended with pure German (the dialect spoken in the assemblies), and the unmixed patois. Out of these three dismembered languages has grown a fourth composed of all the others, similar to the *lingua franca* of the coasts of Africa, which is formed out of the diverse tongues spoken on the shores of the Mediterranean.

But because in German Switzerland there are two languages to be spoken at once—German proper and the patois—it does not follow that they should not be learnt; and because both branches of the German are badly spoken it does not follow that we should neglect the third, the French, which has to be brought into play daily; this, however, happens constantly.

One of the first principles of education is to learn to do well that which one is obliged to do; and as *speaking* is the first object in life, and the most practical, one ought to learn to speak correctly.

The idea which mediocre men, and those destitute of knowledge and taste, entertain of the art of speaking properly is similar to their ideas of personal decoration, the style of which they will ridicule if it is not shaped according to that of their own country. They forget that language is not an ornament but a garb suited to all the emotions of the soul. Who would like to be clothed in filthy and unseemly rags? And if wearing rags that simply hang about the body be loathsome, why should not language—so closely enfolding the spirit according to some philosophers as to be confounded with it—be of vital importance to those who are given to think and to feel?

It is not always in aiming at correct expression, but rather in not thinking of it, that persons skilled in language have produced those masterpieces which, like the letters of Madame de Sevigné, and the fables of La Fontaine, have delighted mankind, and which are more infallibly destined to immortality than works of greater pretension.

One cannot understand how Swiss ladies, generally endowed with so many charms, should attempt to learn music before purging their language of its discordant tones. To succeed in this there should be no hesitation in studying their patois, in order to trace the line of separation between the accents of the two German dialects.

I lament my ignorance of old languages,* and would like to be familiar with the language of my ancestors. But to master a language is to be absorbed by it. The patois being spoken in the councils of German Switzerland, it is very important to have a knowledge of it; I have no doubt that speaking it well would insure more influence and greater advantages in the councils than is generally supposed. A report of debates by Frickhart shows what this language properly cultivated would accomplish in the mouths of Bernese orators.†

* It is known that a patois is simply a language that has been arrested in its growth at a time when the civilization of the people using it became stationary. The use of French by the superior classes of Germany has doubtless arrested the progress of the German tongue. Civilization seems to have borne itself along with the French language, as we see in the case of Frederick the Great, retarding, as a matter of course, the development of the national idiom.

† I question if republican institutions, far from being an

Fifty years ago I heard it stated in Switzerland that the acquisition of a little Latin facilitated the speaking of one's native tongue. Guided by this false maxim people are induced to learn Latin badly, supposing that the little knowledge they may have of it, will enable them to speak their own tongue properly, to the learning of which nobody attaches sufficient importance. And yet these Romans to whom they devote so much study, declare in their best works—*Study your own language!* During the two hundred years that the Swiss have studied the Latin authors, they have failed to comprehend the precepts of Quintilian and Cicero, which, applied to the Germans, mean this and nothing more, *Learn German!*

It is by a knowledge of language that one learns to think, and to develop one's thought. Without a command of language what is called

---

aid in perfecting a living language, do not, on the contrary, oppose its development. Should a member of the council of Berne, as in that of Venice or Genoa, use the polished terms of literature he would appear ridiculous or otherwise not be understood. A republican system serves to develop a national spirit, which is always a benefit, but in obliging a man who thinks to employ the terms of a man who does not think, it retards the natural progress of language.

esprit becomes spiritless and wearisome; sentiment itself would in the long run become tiresome, did it not oftentimes create its own language, always good, as the expression of the heart. Were the letters of Madame de Sevigné written in commonplace French the reader would soon weary of her reiterated expressions of tenderness for her daughter, but which, as given by this remarkable woman, seem to be always new.

A fine mind without adequate powers of expression is discarded by society. In ordinary conversation men affect each other only by the graces of expression, impossible to be preserved in gross and vulgar language. The right word in the right place, the sole merit of expression, is never at hand with persons imperfectly acquainted with their language. Every narrative becomes insupportable in the mouth of a man who speaks badly. Humor, which generally turns on delicacy of sentiment and ideas, being a part of the expression in which it is given, can never live through an imperfect and unfinished language. From the impossibility of expressing gaiety by words arises that gross laughter and pantomimic buffoonery which characterizes the amusements and enjoyment of the lower classes.

It is through the refinement of language that every nation participates in the general progress of intellect. Contemplate the reverence of all ages, and of all enlightened nations, for the Athenians—a reverence, which even in our days consecrates the very soil that gave them birth! When Athens had lost its liberty, it was still protected by the splendor of its name, and consoled for its downfall by the memory of its past glory. It is to its language that Athens owes all these advantages.

I am aware that some instruction in German is given in the greater part of the schools of German Switzerland; but this is not sufficient. So long as a mother is ignorant of the language her child should use, German will always be a dead language for Switzerland. A German theatre would be effective in communicating a knowledge of that language.

* * * * * *

The mastery of a cultivated language raises the man who thinks to the level of the nation itself which has perfected this language. To speak well supposes a habit of attention which is given to the thought itself; moreover, the love of letters cannot be very strong without provoking a desire to write. And if the means of writing are not at hand the love of letters cannot exist, or if existing will soon be extinguished.

I know of few people possessing greater natural talent than the Swiss, especially the Bernese. Were the Swiss to cultivate the German tongue they would soon place themselves on a level with their teachers. In fancying that they were only triumphing over a language, they would really effect the greatest of all triumphs—that of their own talent and mental capacity, now inappreciable through ignorance of a cultivated language.

CHAPTER XV.

LOVE.

IT is astonishing to see how Love in the South creates ideas in the blankest minds. An Italian woman in love overflows with exuberant emotions, and is entirely carried away by the feeling that sways her. Her impulses, chasing each other with the rapidity of lightning, produce varied and consuming fires which prey only on the heart itself. Let love die out in the breast of this woman, and her mind becomes as sterile as the scoria of yesterday's glowing lava.*

In the South Love appeals to the senses, and through them becomes inconstant. In the North it drifts into dreaminess, and oftentimes constitutes the destiny of a whole life. In

* The heart draws its sustenance from the intellect, and being void of impulse it becomes exhausted. We may say that Love has no resting-place in desert hearts.

northern temperaments of this nature the senses are affected only after the capture of the reason. It is but gradually that thought yields to the uncontrollable and mysterious power which sensibility infuses into impulse; the rule of duty is stationary, but its application is constantly changing. Hence the beautiful self-illusions which we undergo when in love, which always result in self-complacency. From this spring innumerable German, French, and English romances, whereof love and the *morale* constitute, nearly always, the staple entertainment, and from which the Italian romances are entirely free. I speak not of the romances of chivalry, in which Love plays but a subordinate part. Compare the romances drawn from the Greeks to the *Nouvelle Heloise* of Rousseau and you will discover the difference between these romances better than I can point it out. If you wish to discover a greater difference still compare Gessner to Théocritus. We behold love in the young maiden of Syracuse, setting on fire all her senses, whilst the mistress of Gessner's young navigator becomes conscious of love's impulse only inductively and by reasonings drawn from the history of birds. In the South love, like a thunderbolt, inflames everything; when at intervals it sheds light on thought it is like the lightning on a stormy night suffusing the whole horizon. If Love in the North burns into enthusiasm it is always through innumerable reasons that it gropes its way to the senses. In dreamy, languid natures the delicate flower of pleasure blooms only in the shades of thought.

Coquetry is born from the union of Love with Vanity. This peculiar hymen is found perfect only in France, where advanced sociability begets an ambition to please by all the means that can secure distinction. The love of Italian women is too intense to be merged into any other feeling; the emotions of English women are cloaked from others through pride; to have love glide into vanity the German woman is too truthful, too honest, or too reasonable.*

When the wish to please is due to the first impulse of love, the art of pleasing reaches that perfection which is still perhaps characteristic of French society. It is only in France that people seek to captivate what they love

* In Germany the term coquetry bears quite an odious meaning, that of a shameless gallantry.

by the graces that distinguish them socially. There is unity of feeling as there is unity of sound. No intoxication is equal to that which arises from seeing a beloved object the cause of pleasure to others; the world then becomes a temple wherein everything is redolent with the incense offered to the object of our worship.

The art of pleasing, as all the fine arts, reaches perfection only through the feeling which actuates and inspires us. Nothing renders us more charming, it seems to me, than a spark of love; and men of mind and taste never more infallibly attain to the art of pleasing than when, carried away by this feeling, they seek to rise in the esteem of those they love by drawing to themselves social distinction. Let us survey all the motives, that is, all the feelings which prompt us to please, and it will be seen that the pleasure we experience is always germane to the feeling which puts us in motion. To please through self-love or vanity is to counterfeit, seeing that we withhold that which we promised. Ambition, when it tries to please, is still more hollow than vanity; there is a chill in simple benevolence, and politeness falls stillborn on the soul, its results being little more than negative.

A charm, to be genuine at its birth, can issue only from a tender feeling, and what is more so than love which alone binds together all the beautiful rays of sensibility. It is the very nature of love to give to manners the witchery and grace which carry us captive, and which no feeling less ennobling than love could replace.

The gift of benevolent expression, born of love, diffuses itself like a perfume over the whole of life. Friendship is dowered with a charm also; it is even an artist, it even moulds new forms, but being shorn of the power of the senses it has less scope than love.

The amiability which we derive from coquetry implies a combination of love and vanity which renders one of them active without absorbing the other. An excess of love renders us indifferent to everything except the object of it, and the disposition to please, impelled only by selfishness, would become dry and barren.

Nothing sins more against the very name of love itself than the notion of some sensualists who degrade the noblest aspiration of the soul to a mere carnal pleasure. Habits and customs grow out of opinions, and the former are constituted by the latter; the virgin soul harbors love only as a sentiment, with the degraded it is but a corporeal need. All are true to their tendencies, and each has a language to correspond; the one that of degradation which is dead to human dignity, the other that of an elevated nature which has conserved all its dignity.

There is no word more profaned than that of Love. What subject has been more overlaid with drivelling and babbling? And yet how fathomless its mysteries! Does it not seem as if our knowledge of any subject was proportioned to the ratio of its distance, since that which concerns us the most is that of which we know the least? We measure the quantities of sidereal worlds, and yet love is a mystery to us!

Our feelings doubtless owe their birth to our corporeal wants; we have all been drawn out of matter. But the dignity of man is due to his development and to his ascension from the material to the immaterial. We now see that his declension is due to his being metamorphosed from a state of dignified thought and feeling to that of low animality from which education and civilization have evolved him.

Contemplate the corrupt ages of Rome and France, and it will be seen that their ideas of love kept pace with the degradation of their manners, and that their theories of love everywhere corresponded to what they practised.

The whole dignity of love is involved in this question: Are we to honor with the name of love the seductions of the senses which we share in common with other animals, even with insects; or if the feeling which all cultivated humanity has baptized with the name of love is not the first instinct of our moral nature, the great motor of all virtue?

There is an ideal in morality as there is in art. This ideal is nature in its pristine state; it is untainted feeling; it is the upright man whom the breath of vice has not yet tarnished; it is, in a word, youth become man, as the rose of a beautiful morning grows with the hours, and expands from its calyx into full maturity. Such is man as cast from the true mould of nature. When love first dawns on his soul his heart cleaves but to what is good and virtuous; his soul swells with the highest aspirations; and if prone to art he will create beauty as it springs from the good and the divine.

What is the well-spring of modesty and

innocence if not the inborn instinct of the two sexes which spurns all love not flowing from the soul, which is not clothed with virtue, without which we are morally neither father nor mother? I would ask every tender soul if in the order of the feelings created in us by love, the cravings of the heart, the yearning for virtue in the cherished object, do not supersede all others? What, moreover, by fallen natures is designated love, is, in a soul on fire with it, the most repulsive impulse if not born out of the heart.

Mystery of mysteries is that great mystery which ushers man into being! In the history of the human heart do we not behold nature striving to substitute the moral for the animal man, a being of body and soul, to think and to feel, and destined for higher purposes than those of mere animality?

Our estimate of women is graduated by that of love. Among the Turks, steeped to the dregs in sensuality, we see the greatest contempt for the unfortunate beings doomed to slavery and maternity. The time was—happily now changed—when France approximated in this respect to Turkey.

It is worthy of remark that esteem for women has never been less than when the most exaggerated phrases of respect have been most current, so much does flattery ally itself with contempt as well in the boudoirs of belles, as in the courts of kings.

CHAPTER XVI.

CICISBEISM.

GALLANTRY has introduced into Italy a species of illegitimate marriage called Cicisbeism, which is much less the result of love than of an indolent disposition common to both sexes. In a country where the imagination rules men court the society of women, especially the younger sons of families, who, excluded by their elders from following a career suitable to their pretensions, pass their lives in participatting the indolence of married women. Society, accordingly, presents the extraordinary spectacle of wives living habitually, to all appearances, with men adopted by them after their marriage.

The evils resulting from this perverted order of things are not where one would at first expect to find them; and female gallantry is the least of the objections to this system of Cicisbeism. The great drawback resulting from it is the destruction of the family. As legitimate husbands never have any but illegitimate children, they cannot love these, while the wives, devoting all their time to pleasure, scarcely have any intercourse with them. Hence the neglect of education, and an improvidence which threatens ruin to all noble families no longer sustained by the laws of primogeniture.

The source of this evil is due to the bad education of women; I will not say of the women of Italy alone, but of the whole of southern Europe. The convent education given them is the worst of all. A French lady informed me that in her youth, on reaching the convent to which she was sent to be educated, the sisters deprived her of all the choice books her parents had given her, leaving her only a book of prayers which she had to repeat in Latin without knowing a word of that language.

Deprive men of the faculty of reflecting by closing to them all the avenues of knowledge and mental culture, and you will see their attention turned habitually on the senses. It follows hence that the soul dwelling, so to speak, in the organs, all impressions will be more imperious and exacting. I remember having been in the apartment of a young lady at the Roman capitol, where for the first time I met her, and of saying to her: "This beautiful prospect must delight you." She answered me quite naturally: "Oh, I prefer this window (giving on a narrow street) from which I can now and then see passers-by." In some of the churches of Rome I have seen celebrated pictures in which the nuns had punctured small holes through which they could see the men who visited the church to admire its pictures. Some ladies who had lived in these convents told me that a young man calling to see these pictures became the object of a violent passion on the part of one of these recluses. Religious education appeals only to the imagination without giving any direction to the mind, and provokes a desire for a paradisaical existence. What would this bliss of feeling, placed in a young heart, be if not that of love? Are not the figures of angels and that of Christ the most beautiful of all forms? What more beautiful than the Christ of Angelica Kaufmann, unless that of the fair Samaritan with whom he is conversing!

Contrast the magnificent temples of Italy

with the churches of the North, where between four dingy white walls, and frequently under the pressure of extreme cold, the most austere morality is preached, and often so ably as to command our best attention and fix the mind by every process of reflection on the necessity of holding our sentiments in proper subjection to principle. Instead of watching handsome young men pass beneath her window the young girl of the North, housed in the paternal mansion, contemplates only the frozen ground, or in her chamber, listens to maternal discourses on domestic economy, duty, morality, and happiness founded on virtue. The tortures of ennui compel the men of the North, confined to their firesides, to read, to think, to love each other, and to occupy themselves with matters of utility. In such a life as this, seductive objects never obtrude themselves to entrap the senses; instead of being busy with the world without, the mind is absorbed with the world within; and when, in short, there is no longer any interest for it in surrounding objects, it buries itself in reflection. In the South, on the contrary, a variety of objects keeps the organs of the senses perpetually active and excited, whereas in the North they become paralysed through the little charm which external objects afford them.*

---

* What is said above of Cicisbeism is no longer of any value, as the French Revolution has entirely changed the face of Europe. For twenty-five or thirty years the attention of people has been, in great measure, given to public affairs, everything else being secondary. When all interest in public matters is withdrawn, the same causes will doubtless again produce the same effects.

CHAPTER XVII.

FRIENDSHIP.

I HAVE sometimes heard the Italians reproached for duplicity, but only by men of the North who are quite as feeble in comprehending Southern people as the latter are in comprehending Northern character. The man of imagination is mercurial, and often in the eyes of the man of reflection appears hypocritical or defective. An Italian, prompted by politeness, will congratulate you agreeably to the exaggerated mode of his country with protestations of friendship which you may take too literally. Is he to be blamed for the inability of others to comprehend his language and politeness?

It may be taken for a general rule that the man of imagination is always an enigma to those destitute of it. The two faculties peculiar to thought and feeling, the imagination and the intellect, are so different in their manifestations that as the one or the other prevails its character is changed. Between the man of reflection and the man of imagination Friendship is seen to be very different. With the man of reflection it is stereotyped into order; with the man of imagination it is rich with exuberant enjoyment, though often fleeting. Everything in formal opposition to principle wounds to the quick the man of reflection, as much as discordant voices of the soul wound the heart of the sensitive.

It is remarkable to see the silence that generally prevails in the social circles of England amongst persons knit together by the strongest ties of friendship. In that lowering climate sentiment and thought, always self-concentrated, seem to be void of language. In a friendship resting on principle there is a calmness, a repose arising from a perfect conviction of being loved, which seems to transform feeling into contemplation. Were this metamorphosis not interfered with by accidental causes which renovate friendship, it would soon decline into an ordinary compact.

In republics where men are constantly either crushed or electrified by the spirit of party, mutual assistance and support become a necessity. This constant need of an offensive and defensive alliance singularly evokes benevolent sentiments, converting friendship into a kind of bond, so much the more sacred that it seems to guarantee public safety and every interest upheld by thoughtful men. I do not know if in England or in America friendships exist between men of opposite parties; friendships of this class, however, are exposed to such trials that they are only to be looked for among men of great integrity.

In a nation eminently social there are conventional friendships (amitiés de convenance) which take the place of the political friendships called by Cicero *amicitiæ forenses.* In France *liaisons de société* have all the external marks of friendship; with ordinary minds they take the place of it, and really promote it amongst individuals worthy of this feeling so common in appearance but rare in reality. These conventional friendships are no longer to be found in the south of Europe. They count for nothing now among women in Italy. It seems that in the South the heart is so interwoven with the senses as to cause friendship itself, as in the republics of ancient Greece, to take too often the very nature of love.

If Friendship were to be estimated according to nationalities I would say that a friendship based on reason is perfect in England, as friendship founded on the imagination is perfect in France. Germany seems to take a middle course between these two nations. Friendship is often as cordial in Germany as in France, but not as much so as in England, where it is constantly renewed by party spirit, and made a virtue through the great interests with which it is connected. In the South, love so absorbs all erotic tendencies as in a great degree to leave no place for friendship. Similar in this respect to exotic plants, Friendship droops in climes where mental culture or fortunate circumstances do not supervene to keep it alive.

A word on the nature of Friendship among men of imagination. With the man of imagination sentiment precedes thought; with the reflective man thought precedes sentiment. We possess a logic of ideas, and are familiar with the laws of analysis, of synthesis, etc. We can analyse complex relationships, and by this course attain to comprehension of ideas, or rather of relationships. All this is as yet locked up within the range of sensibility. The problem of feeling remains so unsolved that although we are constantly using it as a term we are profoundly ignorant of its meaning and tendency.*

I have seen friendships the most perfect spring spontaneously into life, and last as long as connexions the most matured by reflection. It is because the heart is as germane to genuine feeling as genius is to original conception.

---

* The relation of one idea to another is, so to speak, the result of evolution. The idea of a triangle contains within itself the almost infinite relationships of all triangles. But the conception of a sentiment develops no relationships growing out of any meaning attached to that sentiment. We cannot study the effect of one sentiment on another except as in music we study the effect of one sound on another.

To comprehend sentiment demands a faculty of observation capable of rapidly grasping fleeting effects. This capacity is scarcely ever given to great thinkers who are habitually mastered by their faculties of reflection. Geometers, for example, reasoning on certain data, often acquire a tenacity of idea incompatible with the art of observing man's moral condition.

The process of reflection is so opposed to the action of the imagination that one oftentimes excludes the other. In order to maintain a train of thought the action of the imagination is necessarily suppressed. We feel indeed on passing from the chambers of thought to the regions of the imagination as if the mind were setting forth in a new direction, and yielding itself up to new impulses.

The adage of "il faut se connaître pour s'aimer," seems applicable to men incapable of friendship based on the immediate and intimate union of two congenial spirits. The friendship of common minds usually rests on similarity of taste or on a mutual disposition to indolence. Our sentiments are as mysterious as the tones of music. To what sources can we trace those floods of sympathy which have their reason of being in motion? There are even in our moral sentiments deep-seated relations which chance makes known and inspiration unfolds; it is from these relations that arise the cordial and often durable friendships of men of imagination. It is doubtless of these that La Bruyère has said: "There is a point in elevated friendship to which men of mediocrity can never attain."

Intercourse amongst the sexes leads to friendship of a peculiar cast. Whatever in love transcends the carnal senses may be called friendship. With the savage love is an appetite, more fleeting than any attachments amongst most of birds. But as mental culture advances love becomes more and more the gauge of a constant and living friendship. In the friendship that blossoms from love, this first fire of the heart comes from nature; it is nature herself which evokes in two souls the tender melodies which without this first resurrection would have remained silent. It is the resurrection of the soul which seems to determine the nature of our character. There is nothing like first love to elevate or degrade the moral being; did we know how to make the proper use of it, it might become an important means in the education of youth. To waken the heart, to quicken the mind, to arouse the social sentiments, to stir up that yearning for happiness which makes us do so much both for ourselves and others, all this belongs to the first dawn of love, without which man is but a blank, a mere automaton.

Friendship between man and woman has no existence in the South because it becomes too easily transmuted into love. This is much rarer in the North than in France. There is not in the North that delicate essence of love which always renders friendship between the two sexes so intoxicating. Even when the thoughts of love are dead in the soul its memories are always vital enough to hanker after the tender ties whereof all friendship between the sexes is composed.

Friendship between the two sexes is perfect only in France. The Frenchman accessible at all times both through head and heart keeps the avenues of his soul always open; he is pleased through the intellect, and pleased through the heart. The sentiment that would ripen into love in the South is not always in France sufficiently cordial to pass beyond the limits of friendship, while in the North love after a few aberrations lapses into duty. The Frenchman alone is sufficiently electric to emit sparks whenever a woman affects him either through the head or heart. From this affectionate disposition arise manners remarkably social, and which, as a result, never fail to strengthen character.

In the South people remain young too long; in the North they become old too soon. The Frenchman alone, and occasionally the German, placed climatically between the two ages, seem to enjoy both.

The palmy ages of Rome and of ancient Greece were eras of friendship. The polity of a republic and the claims which it has on all its citizens in creating a desire for mutual esteem develops those benevolent sentiments which, assumed at first, finally end in a full realization.

What Ovid has said of love is true of friendship:

Sœpe tamen verè finxit simulator amari.

In aristocracies ambition is a necessary evil, because men in such a state of society are either at the apex or base of the social scale. There can be no principle of equality when the ruling class is at the apex of the scale. The constant desire of ruling over others, or of waging war against our rivals, unfolds to a remarkable degree every desire capable of strengthening the party through whom there is ascent to power.

In antiquity the republican form of government, in drawing men away from habitual intercourse with women, rendered friendship much more common among men than it would seem possible to be in modern times.

* * * * *

The prodigious changes caused by the French Revolution in directing the attention of all men to national affairs compelled women to attend more to their families than they were accustomed to do under the old regime. Family life was the gainer by it, while what is conventionally called society lost by it for a while.*

* In countries where good habits prevailed women appeared

A higher degree of civilization, perhaps, in associating the compulsory duties of the family to the optional duties of society, will link family to social virtues, more important and consequently more binding than we imagine.

The material bearing of everything having reference to the future implies a concordance of its constituents which leads to a final destiny. In morals, where pleasure is an evil only when it is out of place, it is precisely the same. Relatively to the complete development of the social man our affections could never be out of

---

sometimes to have lost the will to please, as if this will had reference only to that which was repudiated by morals. It is with society as it is with the soil—as we sow so shall we reap; its gifts are priceless when one knows how to obtain them, but, neglected, it yields nothing but weeds.

Starting from the principle that there is a fraternal link between man and man, that each is a sound, a reverberation of the great social keyboard, who would not be led to ring harmonious changes on it were it only to avoid the discord and pangs that afflict every man who despairs of himself?

Everything affects the man of sensibility: Living in society we are always unconsciously open to friendship or hatred, to pleasure or pain, to vivacity or boorishness; we are never stationary. The skiff wends its way when the oars are at rest, whilst an imperceptible current sweeps us away to regions of anguish and care.

place, as the accord between our tastes and duties would be such that our pleasures, far from disturbing the social order, would become on the contrary the firmest fulcrum of that order. It cannot be denied that we are on the way to this destiny.

We are disposed to look with too much indifference upon what is called society. It is in society that manners, I might almost say, laws, are formed. With highly civilized nations social reunions are weighty tribunals. It is in order that they may be enjoyed in society that men seek riches and the badges of ambition. The man who feigns indifference to society is seldom insensible to it. Who more sensitive than Rousseau while in the very act of setting at naught the opinion of others? A young man on first entering society becomes virtuous or vicious, stupid or intelligent, according to the impressions he receives from it. It is to society that the man of letters appeals; it is for it that he becomes eloquent. Kings even covet the approbation of society. Did not Alexander make overtures to the Athenians? And if we could recall the ever memorable Athens would it be given over again to a vile rabble by a second Alexander? Every man bows before the final decision of that august tribunal called society.

Let the reader reflect on the wars of the Revolution, on the conquests of the French, on all the upheavals peculiar to that time, and he will be astonished at the humanity of the victorious kings standing in triumph before the walls of Paris after so many cruel and devastating wars. It is to the universal diffusion of intelligence, to French civilization, to the salons of Paris, let it be said, that the humanity of so many victorious nations, restrained and guided by their commanders, is due.

What I term *salon* being but a concentration of dominant opinion, is indeed found among all nations. There are salons in Switzerland, in Paris, and in London; wherever social life prevails, there are combinations of the moral forces of the community fashioning manners, customs, and laws, and controlling the destinies of civilized humanity.

CHAPTER XVIII.

COURAGE.

THE people of the South are the most cowardly or the most courageous of men according to the motive which they may have of being the one or the other. When contending without purpose or reason they are more alive to danger than either the Russians or the Germans; but with a purpose, they will accomplish, with equal discipline and tactics, more than any northern nation is capable of.

From what should the feeling of courage arise if not from the justness of the cause which leads us to expose our lives? If the Southern soldier is badly officered, if he has an unskilful and ignorant general, or if he thinks he is betrayed, he will be painfully alive to the criminality and perfidy of his commander. It follows accordingly that soldiers under an unskilful or treacherous general will be the first to detect that they are badly handled, and the first to relax their efforts. And again, if their leader should fail to show them the justness of their cause, the soldiers of the South would be the first to become discouraged.

The Roman republic was admirably constituted to ensure victory. Love of country deepened in Rome in proportion to the public danger, so that reverses strengthened courage.*

Never did the Roman character attain to a higher standard than after the battle of Cannæ. It was after this defeat—resulting in the cultivation of all the higher virtues—that the beautiful soul of Scipio was formed. From the times of Cæsar down to modern times there is no period in the history of Italy calculated to inspire its people with a high degree of courage. For whom could Italy have fought—under what chiefs and for what rulers? And for what purpose if it was not as Felicaia has said—

Per servir sempre o vincitrice o vinta.

The Italian republics of the middle ages, constituted to inspire enthusiasm, often waged war with hirelings, and to that extent rendered

---

* Livy remarks that the Spaniards displayed greater resources in reverses than any other nation, which is the case in our day.

themselves unworthy of victory. In these trafficking republics military courage, in detaching itself from public virtue, gradually declined. Among the Greeks, especially the Spartans, and in ancient Rome, war engendered patriotism, and patriotism engendered a martial spirit. There being an equality of disciplination everything yields to the enthusiasm of the people of the South, whilst in the North, courage, sustained by reason alone, outlives enthusiasm, it being the nature of enthusiasm to be transitory, that of reason to be enduring.

It is with the military spirit of the two climates as it is with the productions of the earth. In countries where nature seems to furnish everything man becomes negligent; where there is a dearth of natural productions man is fruitful in resources. The loveliest regions of the earth present deserts, poverty, and personal want; in lands where snow prevails there is both abundance and a self-provident spirit, showing that we must seek the priceless gifts of nature in the soul, and that she unlocks her treasures only for those in possession of her golden keys.

In national wars Courage implies a love of the state, and especially of its constitution where there is one. In the last war between the French and the Swiss some of the cantons displayed remarkable courage, not, however, in the defence of Switzerland but in defence of their own districts. Berne, isolated and torn to pieces, fought admirably for its aristoracy; and Underwald, when attacked, displayed a courageous spirit worthy of antiquity. Had the Swiss loved the confederation as the people of the cantons loved their local constitutions, they would have defended themselves in a manner exceeding all expectation. It was thus with the Greeks, who, bound together by no community of feeling, never defended themselves nationally, while the bravery of their separate states is the admiration of all ages.

America, without a constitution, resisted English power through interest in the safety of all, out of which has issued a constitution strong enough to maintain national liberty in combination with the independence of each particular state. The first Swiss Federation grew out of a contingency, and was temporary. No public interest, universally recognised, gave life to the political scheme of an hour! Never did the nation maintain war as a nation; attacked but once, its defence was partial and without unity.

The present union, scarcely adapted to the necessities of internal government, will it provide and maintain the required resources for national defence?

I remember dining with several generals at Milan, at the headquarters of the commanding officer of the French army (Napoleon being at Arcole), when the conversation turned on the fighting capacity of the different peoples with whom the French had waged war. The palm was unanimously assigned to a few regiments of Neapolitan cavalry, who had exhibited more skill and bravery than the forces of any other power. Twenty years later, however, these same Neapolitans showed a great lack of military prowess, because they fought without a purpose. No northern army could have been defeated like these Neapolitans; men of system and reflection never would have abandoned themselves so entirely to the feeling of the moment as these men of the South did.

Should the enthusiasm of Southern people ever be found in combination with good tactics their victories will be equal to those of the French. In long wars, and under skilful leaders, an army becomes a civic body exhibiting all the characteristics of true patriotism. This was the case under Frederick the Great in the seven years' war, during which the soldiers became ardent and devoted citizens of their camps. Wherever and whenever circumstances or accident bring men together for their common benefit, enthusiasm and love of glory will be the natural consequence.

With the Greeks of our day we see a prolonged state of terror gradually harmonizing jealous and barbarous chiefs, resulting in victory and independence to a nation as active and intelligent as oppressed and unfortunate.

CHAPTER XIX.

CONQUESTS.

REGARDED as a body the men of the North have sought, in making conquests, to establish stable communities, and to constitute legislative systems* so conformable to their own character, that to shake their foundations would require a revolution unheard of in the annals of the world.

There is this marked difference between the conquests of Northern and Southern powers; the former grow into nationalities, the latter into segregations. The northern people conquer as a body, and for the benefit of all; the southern people, on the contrary, are but the victims and instruments of those who lead them to victory. Buonaparte's conquests were as personal as those of an oriental despot. In the successive wars waged by him he thought only of

---

* Feudalism.

himself. Always alive to the inferiority of his birth in the midst of the ancient European dynasties, his sole object was to humiliate his rivals. Between him and Alexander there is this difference; Alexander contemplated in his conquests the founding of an empire worthy of a pupil of Aristotle, whilst Buonaparte never regarded his victories in any other light than as contributing to the establishment of himself and family.

CHAPTER XX.

VENGEANCE.

THE most remarkable trait of Southern character is a thirst for Vengeance, a trait especially noticeable among the inferior classes. This baneful passion has scarcely any existence in the North, and forms one of the sharpest lines of demarcation between the two climates.

It is well to state that Vengeance is a passion peculiar to people ruled by the imagination. Every passion checked in its course produces a reaction corresponding to its intensity. The habit of being constantly face to face with external objects, without being attended with internal consciousness, gives the senses a prodigious control, and consequently the passions which they call out. In countries where the administration of justice is slow, costly, beyond the reach of the poor and feeble for all, man thus placed claims the right to defend himself as he best can. Such a state of things leads finally to assassination with impunity. This was precisely the case in the papal states before the revolution and in the Neapolitan kingdom, where the poor assassinated each other without any notice being taken of it by the tribunals.

A thirst for vengeance is so peculiarly the bane of people ruled by the imagination that it prevails amongst all savage nations, with this difference, however, that when the latter become civilized the natives of the North yield to the control of reason much sooner than those of the South who never fully yield to it. There were no assassinations among the ancient like those of the modern Romans. I doubt if an instance can be found either in the histories of Greece or of Carthage, because reflection subjected to law all the passions subversive of society. As I said before, the influence of climate, though constant on man, is graduated by the agencies set in motion by man to guard against it.

The self-control of an irritable man in the North is such that in many duels, for instance those among the Norwegians, knives only whose blades were a certain number of inches in length were used; each combatant held his weapon so as to inflict no deeper wound than that which the stipulated measurement of the blade would warrant. I was assured at Copenhagen that no instances were known of this regulation having been violated, even during the heat of the contest; whilst in Italy the assassin always rushes on his victim in an unarmed state.

Long, I might almost say, perpetual resentment is a distinguishing mark of Southern character. In our mental theories we do not perceive that memory is but the resuscitator of our experiences, and that it always continues the character of the faculty which it represents. The remembered things of the imagination are stamped with passion, those of the intellect with calmness and reflection; we are exhilarated with the remembrance of that which we have only felt; we are soothed, on the contrary, with every thought due to reflection. Hence it follows that the man of the North, more accustomed to reflect than to feel, draws his feelings through his reason, and in thinking of the object of his rage gradually becomes calm. Feeling, therefore, is subordinated to reflection. With the man of the South, on the contrary, feeling, far from subsiding, is ignited by every reminiscence, so that time, which calms down the man of reflection, does but furnish fuel to the man of imagination. In the Memoirs of Benvenuto Cellini we see an almost ecstatic state of feeling, which he records as having experienced on seeing the time approach for the assassination of an object of long-cherished resentment. I know nothing in history which better signalizes the depth of long-treasured vengeance than the detailed narrative of this assassination.

The imperfect system of criminal law in the South is another cause of the thirst for vengeance. In Italy everything seems to favor the assassin. Religion, and in Latium the desert wastes, offer him security and refuge. The all but national thirst for revenge becomes an obstacle to the establishment of good criminal laws, and it but too often happens that the most necessary laws are the last to be established.

CHAPTER XXI.

THE ITALIANS.

NOTWITHSTANDING the great number of travellers who have written on Italy and the Italians there are few people more misunderstood. Like Sancho Panza's geese, all travellers seem to have followed each other in the same track. Pleasure-seekers have lodged in the same buildings, employed the same ciceroni, and retained the same valets; all have been surrounded by the same rogues, male and female, that haunt the resorts frequented by strangers; there have been in every town beaten tracks all leading strangers to the same society.

In France and Germany, and indeed throughout the whole North, mental culture is often the privilege of the nobility, but especially of what was once denominated the *tiers état.** In

* The professional, and the better portion of the middle classes.

Italy the education of the nobility, generally intrusted to lacqueys and monks, was formerly so bad that they were not as a class superior even in manners to the common people. Numerous exceptions to this rule might be found in the larger towns. The few persons of both sexes who have been instructed prove that with equal facilities there is more mind and talent in the South than in the North. The mind of the two climates is like the productions of the two climates—the North has no superiority over the South except that which is owing to labor, method, and perseverance.

In order to see Italy to advantage, and to appreciate the Italians, the traveller should leave the beaten tracks and seek society among those who are not familiar with foreigners; he should mingle with all classes, and sojourn for a time in the smaller towns. During my visit to Bologna I happened to read aloud to a few friends a chapter in Lalande's Travels concerning the character of the Bolognese. My *valet-de-place*, who was present, appeared to listen with great delight. On asking him the cause of his pleasure he replied: "All that came from me—I gave the information!" And he repeated the questions put to him by Lalande and his own responses. I learned through this man that Lalande passed but a few days in Bologna—and yet he ventured to describe the manners, customs, and character of the Bolognese! This is the way in which books of travels are written.

Some men of letters judge the Italians according to impressions derived from reading Machiavelli. The nation has to suffer for the vices of a few among the great, the standard being the atrocious policy by which low, ambitious men, through craft and deceit instead of talent, have sought to maintain their supremacy. In detailing the stratagems of the petty tyrants of his day, as a mechanic would describe a machine, Machiavelli exposed the secret springs of the political life of that epoch. But the picture he gives of these tyrants is simply a portraiture of the tyranny of the feeble, and not especially that of the great Italian nation.

The influence which large towns exercise over smaller ones is less in Italy than in France, where the point of centralization seems to control the entire nation. Hence the success of the Italians in preserving their individuality. Out of Rome there is scarcely an inn to be found: your lodging is in the house of some private individual, who, on the slightest recommendation, receives strangers with unlimited confidence and in the most hospitable manner. I once reached Palestrina (ancient Præneste) at night in company with five or six persons, and before ascending with my carriage into the town, I sent to inform the master of the house at which we were to lodge of my arrival. Although without a letter of introduction, which I had forgotten, we were warmly welcomed by an amiable family, who carried their kindness so far as to let us have the story occupied by themselves. On another journey in Italy I was detained several days by an accident to the post carriage in a town (Macerata) in which I had no acquaintance, and unprovided with letters of introduction. A banker to whom I was an entire stranger, offered and gave to me all the money I required to enable me to continue my journey to Rome.

It is evident from these examples (and I could cite many others) that the Italians do not merit the charge of being distrustful and inhospitable. Like all people led by the imagination they trust those able to inspire them with confidence, and are mistrustful of those that displease them. I have found the Italians generally more disinterested than any other people I am familiar with. I imagine, however, that if they were to deceive they would do so better than people endowed with less finesse.

I believe I observed that people in the North, through a sentiment of benevolence, perhaps of curiosity, are disposed to treat strangers at first sight with great confidence. This confidence is sometimes so blind as to lead to dangerous results through the distrust which it begets.

In the South judgment is often the result of a simple impression; in countries where the senses are less alive than in the South people judge of persons and things according to general ideas. With persons of strong imagination ideas are subordinated to the senses; with men given more to reflection than to the senses ideas take precedence of the senses. It follows accordingly that the first are subject to error, the latter to apprehension and prejudice. A single idea is generalized by the man of imagination. Like the Italian woman he says: All ugly men are without merit; or, like the French woman, the unfashionable man is a fool. A reflective man, on the other hand, sometimes applies a cherished principle to the first case presenting itself without giving it the least examination. Helvetius regarded all men as impelled by selfish interests; Malebranche resolved everything into divinity; and Buffon saw organized molecules as the materialists of our days see ideas in matter.

In the North people like to indulge their prepossessions; and especially to terminate quickly all investigations that require the evidence of their senses. Tropical natures are disposed to judge from feeling, or according to what they imagine rather than according to what they see. To place oneself at the window in order to see what is going on in the street is the last thing, it would seem, that occurs to a Northern nature; whilst the last thing occurring to a tropical nature is to go within himself in order to project himself into the outward world.

CHAPTER XXII.

EDUCATION.

IF a history of Education* were to be written, the art of rearing children would be seen to grow with the growth of intelligence. Among partially educated people parents follow no other guide, in relation to their children, than that of a blind instinct. The idea of shaping a man's character, the power to subject his temper to principle, belong only to the most enlightened parents. Among uncivilized nations children are entirely unrestrained; parents never reprove them, and punish them only

* In Europe the term *Education* has a different import from what it has in America. There the term denotes more particularly the effect of family and social life on individual character, the influence of morals, deportment, habits, and opinions prevailing within family and social circles. It is not, as with us, confused with the term *instruction*, which there commonly signifies knowledge obtained in schools, in professional occupation, and through intercourse with the world at large.
TR.

when in anger; when punished during parental anger the children are rendered afterwards still more wilful by being abandoned to every caprice that belongs to their age.

It is impossible for Northern people to form an idea of the irascibility sometimes encountered in the children of Italy, and especially among Neapolitan children. I have seen one of the latter three or four years old in such a rage that its bite was as much to be dreaded as that of a viper. No angry outburst of our Northern children can give any idea of such a child, nor of the frightful cries uttered in its rage. And yet nothing is comparable to the gaiety of Neapolitan children during their happy moments. I remember passing an hour on the sea-shore at Astura, watching two young half-naked Calabrians about nine years of age and but just landed from a Neapolitan vessel; they were running about on the strand romping with each other and dabbling in the waves of the sea. The antics and sports of our school-boys may be called repose itself compared with the agility and address of these children, and especially when contrasted with the inexhaustibly fertile invention displayed by these little savages.

With such sports and in such a climate we can see how exercises calling upon both mind and body develop the whole system. It is owing to this that the Neapolitans are such excellent models for the sculptor. If the masterpieces of ancient Greece were due to the genius of its artists, the artists undoubtedly owed their models and inspiration to the gymnasium, an institution which could only arise, and maintain itself, in a Southern climate.

Habits of unrestrained freedom, while greatly promoting the growth of the physique, develop the passions to a still greater extent. Children in the South are never obliged to apply themselves to anything requiring close attention, the result of which is that they become incapable of giving attention to anything except to that which strikes their fancy. A child is taken to church, and if it happens to cross the parent's mind a few prayers are taught it and thus its education is finished.

In lands where winter prevails, children are confined to the house for five or six months of the year. Here, under parental eyes, they are more or less affected by the climate, which obliges them to wear close-fitting garments, and to live in circumscribed apartments. The gloom of indoor life and its restraints are more favorable to reflection than life in the open air, and that spirit of independence created by an outdoor life in the South. All constraint, however, whether of body or mind, interferes with perfect physical development. Hence the scarcity of those fine forms north of the Alps which are so serviceable to artists as models. Social necessities, likewise, and the division of labor in manufactories and elsewhere, deteriorate the proportions of the various members of the body. It is with men in society as it is with trees in the forest—each takes the proportions which a little space and the adjoining trees permit, the tree that has plenty of air and sunshine displaying the most magnificent forms and the most luxuriant foliage.

If there are irascible children in the South, the parents are no less so. I have seen at Marino an enraged mother dash her child against a wall and stamp on it until its cries could no longer be heard. Near the house I occupied at Albano, a mother, importuned by the cries of her infant in its cradle, would often beat it until its expiring voice changed to a kind of rattle, which, the first time I heard it, led me to believe that the child was dying. I was told indeed that children frequently die from this treatment. The police take no notice of such things, and the neighbors never meddle with the affairs of others. This want of fellow-feeling in families is a characteristic trait of Southern nations, and is due to the unsocial qualities of their natures and to the habit of leading an out-of-door life.

These irascible Southern parents, when not angry, permit their children to do as they please. So long as these children do not attack each other, they can with impunity attack everybody else, and, in many districts, it is dangerous to trifle with their waggery. We can see accordingly how intercourse between such parents and such children provokes the passions, and how such an education is calculated to check the use of reason.

There are traces visible, but in other forms, of a system of education equally vicious prevailing in the most cultivated communities of the South, and even in the best society. I was one day dining at a certain large town, and the conversation turned on the subject of education. Having remarked that parents in the South of France were in the habit of spoiling their children, there immediately arose such a storm of words against me that I was forced to support my assertion with proofs. A lady present, who sympathized with my views, related in confirmation of them the case of a little girl who, on seeing a companion better dressed than herself, spoiled her frock by pouring oil on it, the act meeting with no punishment whatever from the girl's parents. She mentioned another case, naming both place and persons, of a child who took it into its head to box the ears of an old peasant, who called to transact some business with its father. This child, wishing to carry out its purpose, and finding itself unable to reach the old man's ears, began to cry and to stamp violently on the floor, until its father, to appease it, finally raised it in his arms, and, having obtained permission of the peasant, put the little monster close to his head, and allowed it to box away at its pleasure.

The ascendency which children obtain over their parents is quite legitimate; it is through this they acquire that superior tact and that constant activity which is so peculiar to them. It is an established fact that among all men, and even animals, who live together socially, some eventually obtain supremacy over others by superiority of resources, quite as naturally as fluids varying in specific gravity seek their own level. Perpetually active children, endowed with that nice tact of detecting weaknesses in a superior, always prevail over indolent parents, unaccustomed to the employment of their thinking faculties, and, consequently, deficient in well digested principles.

In the North, especially in Northern Germany, and in Denmark, the education of all classes, but particularly the lower classes, is very carefully attended to. It is especially so in countries where the reformed religion prevails. I believe it is as rare to find men in these countries unable to read, write, and cipher, as it is to find men in the South familiar with these rudimentary branches of education, without which no progress can be made.

In countries where there are serfs, as, for instance, in Denmark, the seignors who are obliged to support them have made it their duty to treat them so well that the abolition of serfdom proves to be much more beneficial to the seignor than to the serfs. Under the régime of serfdom the lands were not well cultivated, and the seignor was the loser. But the peasant, who had no profit in his labor, and who knew that his master was obliged to feed and to lodge him, worked but little and worked badly, even his own soil, so that everybody lost by it.*

Since the abolition of serfdom the seignors follow the noble custom of interesting themselves in the people on their estates as if they were their own children. I have seen, for example, at the residence of the well known family of Reventlow, one of whose members carefully superintends the interests of the peasantry, piles of copybooks sent for inspection by the schoolmasters teaching in the villages of that vicinity.

Religious instruction, it seems to me, is as perfect in Denmark as it well can be. This is a

---

* The peasants had their own portions of land to which they were fully entitled on condition of working the land of their master. This system, in its origin, was the simplest thing in the world. The seignor, instead of paying in money —which he had not—paid for the labor of his peasants in land, of which he had an abundance. The less commerce, industry, money, and population there were, the better the system worked. The peasant was attached to the soil, as the farmer is to his landlord. But when, through the general development of agriculture and knowledge, the resources of labor became multiplied, this régime was found to be inadequate; the lands alike of lord and serf suffered equally, and to such an extent that the abolition of serfdom became a benefit to all.

great advantage, since, independently of other advantages, it is the sole means of anticipating fanaticism, which through the growth of mysticism seems to have spread itself widely over England. An exaggeration of religious ideas leads finally to incredulity, as is apparent in the irreligion of the reign of Charles II., which was brought on by puritanism.

There are two populations in Switzerland, neighbors to each other, the one occupying the canton of Berne, and the other the canton of Lucerne.* The government and the climate of the two districts are about the same, and yet with a soil alike, one is poor, and the other comparatively rich. On sojourning some time in this region I was struck with the disproportionate wealth of the two divisions under apparently equally favorable circumstances.

---

* I know of no population more amiable than that of Entlibuch (Lucerne). A singular custom exists there. On a certain day of the year each village despatches to the neighboring village a sort of herald who announces that on the following day there will be sung to it a recitative of all the folly committed by the said village during the past year. It is rare that any offence is taken at this bit of humor. The verses of these mountaineers are long or short according to the power of the poet's lungs, who takes breath at every *cæsura*. The Lucernese love dancing, and are good musicians

On a closer examination I found that this inequality of wealth had its source in education. In Entlibuch, which is catholic, the people were unable to write or to cipher, whilst in the Bernese Emmenthal, which is protestant, everybody read and ciphered admirably. This single circumstance had sufficed to render the catholic canton tributary to the protestant.

A history of Education would be a fresh and entertaining subject. A respect for this first of all arts would be found to be increasing with the progress of knowledge. Sixty or eighty years ago, in Denmark, the woman who had charge of the children was of less consequence than the one who took care of the hogs and poultry. At present, there is no country in Europe where the advantages of education are better understood than in Denmark. Public institutions and private schools are as carefully attended to there as domestic education. And yet there is perhaps in this country less education among the nobility than among the middle class, which is a great evil.

To the numerous family reunions of Copenhagen, in which all ages are represented, parents are ashamed to bring children badly brought up, which leads them to look carefully to their manners; children even learn to respect each other. I know of nothing so delightful as these reunions of people of every age. These advantages, however, can only be appreciated in countries where people have something to say to each other, which supposes some degree of instruction and broad sympathies, the vitality of which depends on knowledge.

The education of all classes in the South is in the hands of the monks; and although the clergy have not always lagged behind their age, the partial views which they entertain, coupled with their monastic culture, prevent them from being good instructors. I have been amused frequently in Italy, on seeing in the convent corridors the representations of miracles with which the monks fill the heads of the people. A history of these miracles forms a large portion of the element of popular faith.

The only education suitable to children of all ages is the education of the heart; this education is combined naturally with the simplest comprehension of man and his relationships; through it the great principles of all true religion are finally attained.

A capuchin's instruction necessarily leads to fanaticism. The man who believes without a reason cannot sustain himself with one. Intolerance is the inevitable result of a mind that has exhausted its resources; it is owing to this that men become irritated when the opinions of others are different from their own. To give the mind ample scope is to extend the domain of toleration. Monastic institutions not only impart false ideas, but in giving the mind a method inverse to that of the order of truth, render it incapable of forming sound judgments on anything. All the operations of human reason tend to this—to believe nothing for which there is not a sufficient reason. To teach men to believe without reason and against reason is to undermine humanity in one of its divinest gifts, the reasoning faculty.

The religious instruction of the North, in not being intrusted to mendicant monks, gives it immense advantage. So great is the influence of these orders with the people of the South that one may truly regard them as their only instructors. What the various orders of Capuchins are to the lower classes, the Jesuits are to the upper classes; between the two the national mind is deposed, which is impossible in the North.

Gallantry in Italy and in almost all Southern countries, having destroyed many families, the children, especially those of the upper classes, have been but too often abandoned to the care of ignorant, superstitious, and vulgar domestics.

That which in the South renders the education of the people all but impossible is, that the climate allowing the peasantry to be out in the fields the whole year, their children are so occupied there during the day as to leave no time for them to go to school. The Italians are fully alive to the necessity of instruction. I remember that having to settle an account with one of their ostlers I asked him if he could not give it to me in writing. He answered me with an air of pride: "Do you suppose, sir, I would be an ostler if I knew how to write?"

There is a custom of great utility to be found in the South of France, for example at Hyères. The mothers who are obliged to go out to work every day leave their infants with a woman whose business it is to take charge of them during their mothers' absence, for which service they receive the sum of one sou each. This is about as far as the education of the people of Provence has progressed.

I have stated that Education attains to perfection in proportion to the advance of knowledge. Man has made a great advance when he knows how to subordinate his tastes and caprices to principle. Self-sacrifice is not common to the poor any more than it is to the rich. But a good education implies much less the sacrifice of early impulse than it implies fulness of knowledge. There are few good fathers and fewer good mothers who would not adopt with pleasure whatever they believed to be beneficial to their children. There is nothing more difficult than to perceive the relationships between the child that we are educating, and the full-grown and perfect man that we would wish it to be. The father who permitted his child to box the old man's ears would surely have said: "The poor child is ill, very low indeed,—it would not do to irritate it;—such odd fancies as boxing an old man's ears will disappear as he grows older." Moral principles so often give way when brought to bear on things of the heart, that if we do not observe them instinctively, spontaneously, they are gone.

The rich know little of the value of money. The great advantage of wealth is to provide us with means for acquiring knowledge, for with knowledge we possess everything. But this knowledge comes to us only through a complete and finished education. The manufacturing classes are instructed through the manipulation of objects themselves. A manufacturer's son becomes instructed in the fabrications of his father; through a knowledge of them he acquires a fund of information which his parents' example, his energy, economy, love of order and labor enable him to turn to advantage. The workman becomes temperate, prudent, and economical, through the necessity of supporting himself by his labor. Virtue in him is due to his being a workman, while the natural consequences of wealth are indifference, love of pleasure, pride, and frequently contempt for all mankind. Even were the wealthy to escape all these perils in youth, they would not surely escape that indolence which, by all nations, is very justly called the mother of all vice. Nothing, accordingly, but a complete and finished education can protect the opulent man from those vices which attach to his position; naught, therefore, but the best directed effort can place on a level with his advantages, the young man condemned by wealth or rank to every corrupting influence.

I have often regretted that some of the more important principles in the educating of children could not enter into the systems of instruction of both sexes, and especially in that of women. Note the instincts of a young girl: everything tends to make her a good mother, and a good instructress. What care she bestows on her dolls! How she loves to caress and to chide them! How patiently she strives to teach them! Are not these so many indications of the taste of her sex for the office of instructress? Give her children to educate, and see the benefits that will accrue to her. The defects which she cannot see in herself, she will soon perceive in her pupils, and this may lead her to think that she is not wholly free from them herself. Children are, in intercourse with one another, greatly influenced by the behavior of their companions. There is no better time than when this occurs to point out the duty of one to the other; to teach children their proper relationship to each other is not less important than to give them their lessons.

The education which the father of Horace gave to his son has excited the admiration of all ages. Horace's father proceeded from precept to example. Were such a man reproached as a miser, as a libertine, or as a spendthrift, the young poet's father made the son feel how degrading these vices were. Did the virtue of another excite praise, he showed him the advantages of virtue, so that each precept was fortified by a striking example, and to this example was always attached the approbation or contempt of others.

When precepts contrary to the inclinations and self-love of children are directly inculcated, they are never so effective as when the children themselves can be made to see them in their relation to others. To instruct one class of children, through the instruction that should be given to another, would at last end by becoming direct, and this direct instruction would draw their attention to their own conduct; and what is more, becoming fathers and mothers, these same children, instead of adopting haphazard conventional maxims of education, would be in a condition to follow the principles practised and developed in their youth.

Opinions on Education are, in all countries, so fixed that we cannot disregard them with impunity. At Subiaco, a town in the Sabine mountains, I remember having seen in an assembly of ladies, a child about six months old encased in a body of whalebone like a snail in its shell. I could not avoid laughing at the sight, and afterwards pitying the little martyr. It would be hard for the reader to realize the indignation of the mothers against me; and when their indignation was over they became so eloquent in showing me the necessity of their course that, on leaving them, I was disposed to believe that an infant without a body of whalebone would probably fall to pieces, seeing, according to the views of those ladies, that the backbone would break like glass.

The majority of men even of those called reasonable, are controlled by the prevalent opinion of the town or country in which they happen to dwell. In the South of France it is a common thing to hear mothers say that there is only one happy period in life—that of infancy; and that children must never be robbed of this by constraint or control. This maxim is taken literally from Rousseau, without any knowledge on the part of those who use it, that Rousseau's work *Emile*,* from which it is taken,

* "Emile" introduced some beneficial changes in the early treatment of children. It discredited the absurd practice of

is wholly opposed to anything of the kind. Before Rousseau became in France an authority in educational matters, it was but too common to punish children. We have reason to believe that when the punishment of children was sanctioned by public opinion in France, those who now spoil and pamper their children, would then have punished them, so little hold has reason upon men, most of whom have but merely borrowed ideas of her.

Education in early times and amongst all people was confined to the family, and each family living away from all other families, the education of children consisted of nothing but an imitation of what was seen amongst the parents; at a late period it would seem that each family gradually took the particular turn

---

swaddling infants like mummies, to the manifest injury of their tender limbs; it induced mothers of the higher ranks to suckle their children instead of committing them to the care of nurses; it corrected several wrong principles of early education, such as that of ruling children through fear, of considering them as slaves having no will of their own, and of terrifying them by absurd stories and fables; it inculcated freedom of body and mind, the necessity of amusement and relaxation, of appealing to the feelings of children, of treating them like rational beings. Rousseau may be truly called the benefactor of children. *Gallery of Portraits.* Tr.

which each profession adopted. We see in the comedies of Molière that there was a time in France when all classes and professions in society had marked habits, manners, costumes, and a distinctive language.* The lawyer, the courtier, the soldier, the physician, the partisan, the devotee, without including Messrs. Purgon, seem to those of the present day to be caricatures, whilst in their generation they were so many living portraits. We see that comedy was supplied with characters already formed in the times of Molière. Good comedy issued naturally from the sharp contrasts presented by so many distinct classes of men. The habits and costumes with which each class was labelled, so to say, necessarily affected personal character, which at that time was more strongly defined than at present, just as a wild animal possesses more defined characteristics than the same animal domesticated. Again, the sharply defined manners of the age of Molière were

---

* The first thing the spectator notices [in the middle age period] is the distinction of the several classes by their several costumes. He can tell at a glance the calling of a man from the color and other qualities of his dress. The gentleman is not confounded with the trader, nor the pert apprentice with the finished craftsman. *Secularia.* Tr.

better adapted than those of our day to comedy of the school of Plautus and Aristophanes, which seems to have arisen in an age equally as prolific in caricature as that of Molière.

One of the remarkable effects of education in modern times, especially in France, is thus noticed by Montesquieu: "We receive," he says, " three descriptions of education, that of our parents, that of our tutors, and that of society; what we are taught by the latter overthrows all ideas derived from the former."

In France, more than anywhere else, a young man found in society the instruction which was to guide his future life. Whatever advantage this species of education possessed is due to the eminently social qualities of the French, who better know than any other nation how to diffuse their ideas. A rapid circulation of ideas is for the mind what a specie currency is for commerce, a reliable source of wealth. Rarely are ideas or money interchanged without profit.

The necessity in France of being easily understood in conversation, prompts thinking men to impart great clearness to the ideas which they put in circulation.* It happens accord-

* A great deal is said about the perspicuity of the French language. It is not necessary to commend this language for

ingly that these ideas enter rapidly into circulation, and finally become current through the use which is made of them.

---

its perspicuity, since all languages demand the same attention in this respect as the French. The lucidity of French authors is due to the social qualities of the nation, and not to the language itself; it is their sociability which has made their language a circulating medium for all refined people. Scientific terms are excluded from it; logical formulas and labored processes of reasoning are also avoided; long phrases are rarely tolerated, these being reserved, very properly, for passionate outbreaks. Tedious periods, like those of the German, the Latin, and the Italian languages, with the verb at the end of the sentence, to bind together a group of incidental phrases, are contrary to the impatient spirit of conversation.

This spirit is essentially dependent on tact; it supposes a quick perception of that which inspires conversation, and of that which demands silence; it supposes a mind capable of attending to two things at once, the subject itself, and the sentiment of the speaker. Women, and sometimes great men, are remarkable for this twofold capacity. It excludes long phrases, as being better calculated for the tribune than for the *salon*.

The great sociability of the French nation naturally gives a conversational form to its language, and as language exercises a secret influence on ideas, it serves in its turn to render the nation sociable.

No language is richer than the French in conversational material; none possesses such a fund of well-turned phrases; we also see, in almost all European countries, that ceremonial terms, and everything belonging to polite society, are expressed in French phraseology.

The habit of frequenting social circles had on the youth of France a singular effect, particularly on their manners.

Another cause of the perspicuity of the French language is owing to the general prevalence of conversation, which gives the inappreciable advantage of testing the effect of one's phraseology, an effect that never can be imagined if one has not experienced it.

In order to insure the success of a work in France, it must be put, so to say, on a conversational footing with the nation. The verdict of society in Paris is the law of the empire. To secure readers a hearing must be obtained of the judges presiding over this tribunal, who are at once the leaders of society and the umpires of perspicuity in ideas and expression.

Where social tastes, however, are too exclusively prevalent in a nation, language deteriorates through the limited range of ideas that are current in what is generally called society, that is to say, it becomes impoverished.

This impoverishment is one of the causes of obscurity in a language, since the fewer its terms the more do the significations of a single term augment. The context and other collateral aids have to be brought forward in order to arrive at the meaning of the term made use of, thereby adding another difficulty to all the others. Again, some caprice, some particular fancy of a clique, fashion, in fine, may prescribe certain valuable terms, or introduce others solely to express the ideas of a coterie. The improper use of pronouns is another cause of obscurity; these sometimes beset one like traps in a discourse, as if to keep one constantly on his guard, the reader's situation being somewhat like that of a workman compelled to operate with an inferior instrument.

It must not be supposed that politeness consists only in matters of mere ceremony. True politeness has its source in the best qualities of the heart. It teaches us to restrain envious passions; it creates a habit of thinking of others; it excludes everything that can wound the feelings; it teaches us to forget ourselves, and the expression of esteem for others is all ready either in act or word. The language of politeness can be in its origin only the expression of genuine feeling; when it ceased to be an expression of true feeling its form was preserved both in manner and word.

When at a later period virtue was jeered at, men degenerated into scoffing and ridicule, and while assuming the garb of regard and respect, secretly inflicted injuries on those least expecting them. In short, the fatal flaw between corruption of manners and expressions indicative of virtue gave rise to sinister thoughts and robbed language of its mission and true import.

When the whole French social system crumbled at the Revolution every factitious element in society disappeared with it, and every man returned to his natural proclivities. Out of this order of things good arose to some and evil to others, society remodelling itself, not according to still undefined usages, but according to the transient phases of the Revolution and the characteristics of individuals. Language, manners, habits all had to be recast. But as the intellect of the century, far from being extinguished, was everywhere paramount and untrammelled by impediments, intelligence and manners gradually advanced, either through the death of old superstitions, or by what the mind, enlightened by experience and the generally diffused knowledge of the times, could add to them. One of the leading effects which this general convulsion produced, was to banish more or less all its dialects, by subverting in language, as in manners and customs, almost everything that pertained to France before the Revolution. The conscription everywhere established, and war declared against all nations, by banishing dialects left everywhere traces of an improved language; the desire to read grew with the increase of readers, and newspapers became, almost throughout the globe, one of the necessaries of life.

I have to add a word on the subject of national instruction.

A true system of national instruction, the

only serviceable one, is that which confines itself to imparting knowledge appropriate to every man's pursuit. It is important that the laborer and the farmer should understand agriculture, the gardener gardening, the shepherd sheep, and the wine-grower the culture of the grape. Instruction of this kind is alone profitable to the people, because it alone relates to a class of ideas preliminary to each calling. It is only on such a foundation, already prepared by education and by the necessities of life, that the rudiments of useful instruction can be laid. A husbandman acquiring some knowledge on a model farm will profit by it in subsequent labor; he will get into the habit of analysing the nature of his work; his knowledge extending itself more and more, will render his occupation more and more pleasant and necessary to him. It is the knowledge that is gained by us in our own calling that will profit each of us in everything within our own jurisdiction.

Those who think there is danger in instructing the masses, always imagine that the instruction given them will lead them to reason on matters beyond their comprehension and foreign to their calling. The best means of preventing this evil is not to allow their ideas to run at random, but to direct the knowledge of each in accordance with the demands of his condition. To suppose that men's thoughts can be in one direction, and their occupations in another, is to reverse the order of things. Our object should be to confine the knowledge of each man to his peculiar calling, to fasten his ideas to the duties of his condition, and in this way give greater stability to the social system.

The absorbing topic with the masses is how to provide for the necessities of life. A man unintermittently devoted to gaining his own livelihood will always take an active interest in whatever tends to improve his condition. Any instruction that appeals to this end will be the most profitable to him. It is in itself a source of happiness, and it is in the enjoyment it provides that pleasure is always found in harmony with duty. All true pleasure flows from a source like this, and the life of man is not completely happy or tranquil without it.

That which constitutes the wealth of a nation is not a few perfect farms, a few examples of superior cultivation, but a universality of good cultivation, one that implies intelligence universally diffused; as bread is necessary to every village so are the means of instruction necessary to every man.

In respect to the masses there can be no mistake in this principle, that *useful instruction is the basis of moral instruction.* It is the instruction suited to the calling of each that gives to man those ideas of order which are the foundation of justice and the source of morals. The individual, quite as much as the nation, has his measure of ideas. Ideas which tend not to order, tend to disorder. To what use would you have man devote his activity if not to the good to which he attaches it! Ignorance is not altogether due to the absence of thought, but is, on the contrary, often due to the activity of thought abandoned to chance, so frequently destructive. Seditions and revolts frighten people, but are not these traceable to popular ideas which are at the mercy of the passions, and which interfere with the consolidation of society?

* * * * *

As a conclusion to this long chapter I shall state that the great difference between the education of the man of the North and the man of the South is this, that, with the former it is the result of reflection, and with the latter it is due to external objects.

The man of the South will sooner attain a high degree of civilization than the man of the North; but the slower advance of the man of the North will infallibly enable him to arrive at rational principles. The result of this is that imagination develops itself faster in the South, and the faculties of intelligence in the North.

The man of the North, in neglecting his education, will degenerate faster than the man of the South, who will never be without the education of the outward world, and that of the passions.

In the North the book of nature is closed the greater part of the year, whilst in the South its most attractive pages are always open for man's perusal. Among the civilized nations of the North the long winters are devoted to the analysis of thought, whilst in the South every month of the year is calculated to seduce the imagination with its beautiful images.

In the South civilization ebbs and flows rapidly. The civilization of the North, based on principle, is slower in its march, but, owing to a combination of science and reason, is infinite in its flight.

CHAPTER XXIII.

THE INFLUENCE OF CLIMATE ON HUMAN SENTIMENTS AND HAPPINESS.

IN countries where the imagination rules ideas flow more rapidly than in countries where the habit of reflection prevails. With men given to the imagination feeling is married to the senses; with men given to reflection it is closely allied to reason. In Italy one is loved according to his ability to please; our early predilections, in the North, are also due to the senses, but as we are under the dominion of reflection, it is imperative that the head should sanction the impulse of the heart. To break a tie in the North we must unravel in thought the threads of the affections; in the South they become detached through the senses. Hence it is that in the North the sentiments are a subject of endless discussion, while in the South to make feeling a matter of discussion is very rare.

Habits of reflection in the man of the North generate moral qualities which tend to render the affections permanent. The tenacity of feeling which results, therefore, is doubtless a blessing when carried into love and friendship, but when carried into checkered feeling is a great misfortune. Feelings of an agreeable nature, particularly those denominated *pleasure*, are fleeting, while it is the very nature of sorrow to be more lasting than pleasure. This order of nature, in itself, is to be deplored; but what is still worse, is, that when the feelings of sadness are long increasing on the one side, the capacity to enjoy pleasure decreases on the other. I have often observed that persons of a reflective turn of mind who have suffered much, become insensible to agreeable emotions, regarding them apparently with aversion. This disdain of pleasure, however, which they affect, is but incapacity to feel it; to propose diversion to such minds is like proposing to a sick man to dance.

Many false notions grow out of the inability to entertain agreeable sentiments.* Thought

---

* There is no essay known to me which contains more truth, than that on Happiness by Fontenelle. That portion

generally follows the bent of our humor—our peculiarities of feeling,—or, rather, is controlled by the dominant sentiment which inspires it. In this dominion of sensibility over thought amongst sad and reflective persons, we often discover systems of gloomy ideas as destructive in their effects as they are false in their principles. As we often see bats nestle within lofty gables so do the most distorted conceptions often seek shelter in the dark corners of the most exalted ideas.

The true antidote to this morbid humor (which frequently assumes the mask of reason) is reason itself. A dreamy temperament is owing to a peculiar structure of the nervous system; now it is the province of reason to guard our ideas from its undue influence by modifying the range of the imagination.

The mind naturally inclines to that which best promotes its activity. In the North, where

---

of Happiness which is in the power of man to attain, is composed of petty enjoyments within the reach of all and in every situation of life. By bestowing thought on pure and accessible pleasures there is ever a growing appreciation of their value. And what is of still more consequence, a relish for agreeable sensations is never lost. The effect of this is to preserve the heart and mind in a healthy tone, without which there can be no happiness.

outward objects present few attractions, the mind gives itself up to inward contemplation; when this becomes incoherent it is idle fancy; when it is employed methodically, and free from the caprices of the imagination, i becomes reflection.

To think is a pleasure in the North. It is the necessity of every reasonable being in such a climate. The inhabitant of the North, instead of looking for objects of enjoyment without him, descends into the recesses of his own nature for his enjoyments. Outward objects constitute the happiness of the man of the South; the inhabitant of the North finds it within himself. Like a butterfly, the man of the South lives on the nectar distilled daily from the flowers that grow on his own soil; while the man of the North, on the contrary, is the diligent bee who nourishes his mind on that which he has garnered in seasons of sunshine and bloom.

Social relationships are paramount in countries where nature, during half of the year, has no life for man. Whatever in such climates is not appropriated to the demand of the outward world is consecrated to social communion. It follows, therefore, that the study of man and his social relationships takes root much sooner in the North than in the South. Men are consequently closely drawn together by the necessities of life and the need of mutually assisting each other.

It is a Northern poet, in a poem rich with sublime thoughts, who declares that

> "The proper study of mankind is man."

No knowledge so absorbs and satisfies the soul as knowledge of oneself. Whilst every other study makes us forgetful of life, the study of ourselves renders us mindful of it. A man accustomed to self-observation, discovers in himself phenomena which light up the very recesses of his being. We see the pleasure of the botanist on discovering a new plant, and the transports of the philosopher on discovering a great law of nature. But these satisfactions, though rare, are found outside of ourselves, while a study of oneself furnishes an inexhaustible source of delight springing from the very centre of our being. Systems are constructed by the naturalist, by the man of science, but they are not his dwelling-place; the heart has no allotment in such mansions, whilst a knowledge of ourselves lives with us like a bright luminary for ever cheering and warming us. In addition to the science of the naturalist, of the chemist, of the man who studies other things than himself, there may be a character feeble in will and weak in principle—one who, when requiring the forces of his own soul, is a stranger to them from never having courted familiarity with them.

In the consciousness of moral and mental power there is an inappreciable enjoyment, as there is in the discovery of all psychological truth. When the art of self-observation is mastered, man discovers in himself a continent, an unknown world in which he may conquer everything he desires for his own benefit. This study serves him in all times and in all places; it enables him to dispense with society and with books; it alone reconciles him with his kind by constantly reconciling him with himself. To live harmoniously with our fellow-creatures is, with most men, an accident, whilst it should be an object of study. We agree or disagree with each other according as we know how to maintain ourselves in harmony with each other's sentiments. These laws of social concord must be sought for in ourselves, for our self-relations are no less varied and complex than our relations to others; we are good or bad companions to ourselves according as we know how to live well or ill with the laws of our interior constitution. Life, indeed, is but a body of necessities and desires, gratifications and discomforts rapidly succeeding each other, and ever reviving in new and diverse shapes. To these conditions of our sensibility correspond our thoughts, which appear and disappear according to the mysterious needs of our consciousness which is ruled by the imagination.

Happiness proceeds from the harmony which is maintained between this action of thought on the one side and that of sensibility on the other, both of which inward movements are apparently vague and irregular, but really are as subject to inflexible law as all terrestrial phenomena. The study of these laws, which constitute the destiny of man, is of all studies the most neglected!

An ignorant and vulgar man is ignorant and vulgar with himself; his vulgarity displays itself as much in his own person as in the society of others. Without constant self-watchfulness, and the steady exercise of our reason, we undermine our own individual respect. We often forbear speaking to others of that which is painful to them, and yet indulge thoughts and reflections in our own breasts which are ruinous to us. All the observances of society, all those which make our intercourse with others pleasant or painful, can well be applied to oneself. This is easily understood. We belong to society through the same necessities and the same ties that belong to our own feelings.

As the other sciences are, so is the science of humanity, which is uncertain and erring in its very incipiency. I will not say that error is an avenue to truth, but it is a road which must be travelled in order to attain gradually to useful and permanent results. Physical science was, at its birth, but metaphysics, astronomy but astrology, and chemistry but alchemy.

It is the same with the science of man. We have to grope through errors a long time before we ascend to the moment when one truth becomes the parent of another. As yet we have scarcely an idea of the great classes of phenomena which may shed some light on the nature of our existence. Memory and imagination are still confounded, and no one has yet clearly separated the imagination from the intelligence. There is an imperfect comprehension of the correspondence between the phenomena of organization and the laws of thought, and yet they are interchangeable. At one time, natural philosophers deny the existence of the soul; at another, we have dreamers who deny the existence of bodies. The mystics seek to be free from the influence of the imagination, whilst men of the world, of the Epicurean class, deny the power of reason.

The true principles of morality are yet to be discovered along with a more correct knowledge of the faculties of the soul.

It is commonly believed—and a great mistake it is—that the natural sciences enable us to dispense with a knowledge of ourselves. There is a point in the highest regions of the natural sciences where the theory of the facts becomes so abstract and ideal that it can be controlled only by a more advanced knowledge of the instrument of thought itself. It would seem that chemistry has already reached that advanced point when it requires metaphysics rather than facts to guide it.* Method is to science

---

* A chemist of forty years ago [the time at which our author wrote], well versed in the subject as it then stood, would be utterly lost in the new names and facts, and new

what machinery is to the industrial world; as the spinning-jenny draws out thread so does method guide thought. Our inward perceptions, however, are still so confined that we often mistake one wheel for another; it becomes us, therefore, if we would attain to any perfection in the highest regions of science, to study the instrument we employ, that is to say, become familiar with the faculties themselves of thought, and of the laws of their development.

There is no study that has greater attractions than that of moral philosophy. The laws of our existence unfold themselves before us from the moment that we know how to observe ourselves from a proper point of view; when this takes place we cease to stand alone, and to be alienated from ourselves. All our moral destinies yield to the empire which we form within ourselves. The thought which hangs solitary in the brain of the man ignorant of himself, becomes a twofold charm to him who has acquired a knowledge of the conditions of his own existence. In learning to realize the laws

combinations, which appear in the works of the present day. Sir Henry Holland. 1862. Tr..

of our own vitality, we become cognisant of the various noumena, which make up our being, and to which we hold for good or evil by various ties. The harmony of all these interior forces is but another word for happiness. The first condition of self-knowledge is that of probing our own consciousness. To do this effectually we must not be haunted by exterior influences; a retired spot is necessary for meditation; secret thought disappears before the light of the sun. It is thus with all strong impressions; they gradually efface the perceptions of our inward world, and banish all self-scrutiny.

The secrets of our own souls are destined to come to us from the gloomy climes of the North. The sweet feeling of repose is born from-cooling sensations, whilst the feeling of heat, when not excessive, leads to motion. We must seek moral philosophy in the North, its true birth-place.

We see in the poems of Ossian, in the Scandinavian mythology, and at a more recent period in the visions of Scotch and English mystics, and in the philosophical revelations of Kant, a disposition at one time to idle fancies, at another to contemplation, fruitful in poetry, in truth, and in varied projects. Let a sound philosophy be propagated throughout this land so rich in thought, and the most sublime conceptions will be seen to flourish in these regions of snow and fog, and shed brilliant light over the climes of the South.

Let not the English forget the times of Charles I. They ought to dread more than they do those mystic vapors which, like storm-clouds, are raised up, and massed together on all sides. It belongs to the thorough study of moral philosophy, and especially to a sound theory of the imagination, to dispel these sentimental visions which, on the appearance of certain truths, as the nature itself of the thinking and cognisant being, take flight. It would have been time lost to have undertaken a few centuries ago to refute the astrologers; since the advent of astronomy astrology has given way without a struggle, like the disappearance of darkness before the light. It is never by battling against error that we overthrow it; it is by enlightening man, who is the seat of it.

If the Fine Arts are native to the sunny skies of the South, *moral beauty*, by way of compensation, is native to the North. As in northern climes the aurora borealis is sometimes a substitute for daylight, so moral beauty often compensates the man of the North for the absence of that artistic enjoyment which his clime seems to deny him.

Music has its source in the folds of our sensibility. We are at one time in, at another out of harmony with the feelings of others. But as the tone of our feeling is constantly varying, harmony at best is but momentary, and often the result of accident. It was thus with musical harmony before the science of music was born. The harmony, however, of our own interior forces always exists. Centuries succeed one another, nations appear and disappear, without taking from men the art of adapting themselves to each other. It belongs to moral philosophy, to a sound theory of our sentiments, both being founded on a correct colligation of facts, to discover the laws of unity between cognate beings. This sublime unity, in annexing itself to ideas of order, of principles, and of virtue, seems to be allied to those laws of supreme wisdom, which in the eyes of the soundest philosophy govern and rule the universe.

The true philosophical spirit is that of the observer. The observing spirit applied to oneself is an indwelling light, which, although lighting up our inward darkness, adds life to the will; whilst the study of objects exterior to man never reaches down to the motive principle of human action. Hence, we see men often become great through external circumstances, who in themselves, that is intrinsically, are worthless.

The transport of the senses under the burning sky of the South often renders the inward thought dead. It thus happens that the man of the South, under the dominion of external nature, does not know, like the man of the North, how to rule his life by stringent principles. If we are to assign greatness to the men of antiquity, we must do so rather in view of their passions than their principles.

Not to suffer is to be happy in Northern climes; the absence of pain there is enjoyment. When we hear the moaning of the wind, when snow-flakes thicken the air and carpet the earth, the father of a family, whose enjoyments are all drawn around him, is content with the roof that shelters his wife, his children, his hearthstone, and his home. Such a man is qualified to indulge in the pleasures of hope, and to live in the domain of thought; the less nature gives, the more he delights in his family, in the resources of his mind and heart, and in all surrounding objects. In the South, on the contrary, the absence of pain is less felt. Pleasure abounds everywhere, and is always man's chief object. The man of the South, placed like a king of the universe under the canopy of an ever serene sky, daily revelling in flowers and fruits, dazzled with the éclat of life, and intoxicated, not with ideal, but with sensual gratification, has no distant future to anticipate, or remote past filled with cherished souvenirs, to supply to him the charms of his existence. In the midst of nature's bountiful gifts, ever the subject of keen sensations, and exposed to all the risks of a life not maintained by self-exertion, he is destined never to live with himself and enjoy the benefits of self-communion. The man of the North, on the other hand, endowed with the sublimest of all gifts—that of directing his own destiny—proves to us that human dignity, as well as power and happiness, resides in thought and in reflection far more than in any other agency that ministers to the progress of our race.

CHAPTER XXIV.

WHAT WE HAVE BEEN, AND WHAT WE ARE, OR 1789 AND 1894.

THE foregoing chapters consist of the reminiscences of my varied life; I have painted the manners and morals of nations as I have found them. Most of the pictures thus given belong now to another condition of society, to a former era, to an epoch beyond the grand historical barrier called the Revolution; almost all have disappeared, leaving but fragmentary portions of that which can no longer be restored. The Alps are seen to separate people who bear no affinity to each other. Thus is it with that great revolutionary cordillera dividing off two centuries, separating men so different that people like myself, who have lived during both epochs, are astonished to find ourselves unchanged.

Is it not strange that not only the French, but the European people generally, have lost to a greater or less degree the institutions possessed by them before that event? And yet this revolution seems to be foreign to nations which opposed it! Let us take the French as an example, that we may see the transmutation which they underwent, and what is true of them is not the less so of their imitators.

The sword on one side, and the chapeau under the left arm—these relics of ancient chivalry, these tokens of respect and of slavery to beauty and rank—have disappeared, together with hair-powder and superfluous lace; habitual forms of exaggerated esteem have given way to the simple and natural language of the heart, and to what is appropriate; with the veneration for the great has disappeared all contempt for the humble. Whatever of servility that once entered into the respect for women, is now replaced by esteem or indifference; women are now addressed like men, being spoken to or neglected according to the merits, charms, or mental accomplishments, which it may be supposed they possess. Beauty despoiled of coquetry remains as a simple souvenir—it concerns us no longer to think of it. Men and women commingle in the *salon* as if they were of two diverse nations, each speaking the language peculiar to himself or herself. Hence his neglected toilet, those loose *negligé* pantaloons; black clothes of the finest cloth, and of remarkable neatness, constitute all the luxury of modern attire. With unpowdered, uncurled locks, a head of the present day bears some resemblance to the heads of antiquity.

What vain speeches, what useless formality, what affectation and ceremonial mockery, have disappeared with the towering head-dresses and expanded skirts of the women of former times! What deferential observances and spurious compliments are gone with the small-clothes and frizzled heads of the men! What conventional flattery and superannuated pretensions are laid aside with rouge! What remnants of a false and barbarous taste lie buried and forgotten along with the hoop-petticoats of our great-great-grandmothers, and the enormous perruques of our grandfathers!

Let us see what constitutes the new order of men.

The French nobles of the ancient régime, despoiled by the Revolution of their titles, wealth, and hopes, found themselves reduced each to his own personal merits. The road leading to fortune, and all the avenues to ambition, being closed, how did they bear the burden of their numerous misfortunes!

Holding various offices in my own country at the time of the Revolution, and brought in contact with large numbers of French emigrants, and having opportunities to observe them closely, it was a matter of surprise to me to see how many useful qualities they possessed, accompanied with the agreeable habits and manners so characteristic of that nation. Determined to be happy with the people around them—an essential point in the art of pleasing—they enjoyed everything, and were proud to be content with an exile which, fortunately for them, they believed would not be long. The absence of resentment and despondency, their natural gaiety, sometimes in the depths of poverty, while rendering them agreeable to others, rendered them not less so to themselves. I have seen M. Le Noir, formerly Lieutenant of Police at Paris, cheerfully mount a peasant's cart in order to journey to a neighboring town, and his journeys were rarely without instruction to himself and to others.

How strange it is that these emigrants, who estimated people with whom they were compelled to live so truly, could never comprehend the men and the society of their own country. Their regrets for what they had lost so intensified their souvenirs of their native land, as to render them incapable of appreciating anything apart from that which they themselves once enjoyed in it. From this resulted the singular anomaly of persons, clear-sighted in respect to what was novel, but utterly blind to that which concerned themselves. A similar phenomenon was indeed observable amongst men of every country in Europe, holding at this time any prominent position; all judged the Revolution unwisely; all were clear-sighted in relation to past events, but more or less blind in their views of the present. The ability to perceive the transient, the judgment to estimate the future, are they gifts refused to those in high places? Or is the sentiment of man's power such as to make him think he can command time itself to stand still for his especial benefit?

It was a remarkable thing to see in France, and in all countries under French rule, men of all classes stripped of everything factitious and conventional. There was intercourse without ceremony, and conversation without that commonplace verbiage which is so convenient for people who have nothing to say; people would accost each other with thoughts and not phrases; no one entered society, not even that of the Emperor, without finding himself immediately in earnest conversation with him.

A mission fulfilled in the Italian portion of Switzerland obliged me to make repeated journeys to Milan (in 1795–6–7). How great the contrast between the inflated, pompous display of the officials of the Swiss cantons, and the prompt decisive action of the men of the *Grande République!* At Milan I was presented to the Proconsul, at that time almost a king in Lombardy, representing the people of * * * * This potentate received me at the top of a staircase without coat, vest, stockings, shoes, or pantaloons, in fact, in his shirt, and almost naked. I could not refrain from smiling in contrasting this African costume with the bands, and wigs, and long full robes, enveloping my Helvetian neighbors. It gave me pleasure to converse with the French soldiers. On inquiring of a general if it was allowable to put questions to them, and on receiving a favorable answer, I went so far as to demand of one of them why the war had been carried into Italy;—"In order to have no enemies at home," he replied with peculiar energy. On mentioning General Buonaparte, they smiled complaisantly as if I had spoken of a mistress. To illustrate the high opinion which they entertained of his courage, one soldier told me that the general would not advance his right foot before his left to save his life. I cannot conceive of a more perfect combination of liberty and obedience, nor imagine a discipline more free from pedantry than that which was displayed by the army of Italy. The terrible war in which it was engaged seemed to it to be a party of pleasure. There was no dread of fatigue or suffering; enthusiasm reached its highest pitch. A soldier had lost a leg, and whilst the wound was being dressed I approached his bed, as if attracted by sympathy, and exclaimed, "You must be a great sufferer!" "Ah, citizen," he replied, "suffering is nothing when a man suffers for his country." What could not be accomplished, and what was not accomplished with men of this stamp! The politeness of the officers of this army was a model of that natural politeness which characterizes the new régime. In the absence of conventional forms the goodness and cheerfulness of the young heroes seemed to stand forth in bold relief.

Abandoning details, however, let us glance at the general effect of the Revolution on all European nations, and especially on the French.

Previous to the Revolution every man lived by himself within the circle of his own interests, pleasures, and individual cares, without reading his fate in the public journals, or in the passing events of the day. At that time kings were similar to the gods of Epicurus, seemingly indifferent to the fate of all created beings; only a few of the Olympian order being allowed to enter their presence, the rest of the human family fulfilled their destiny as best they could. Ideas of public welfare had no existence, since man's destiny was confided to the hands of a few ministrants exclusively qualified to do as they pleased with the millions of mutes for whose benefit they were specially created. No man had conceived of morals as forming a subject of public interest; vice was avoided solely from motives of personal calculation. If by chance the eye fixed itself on the courts of kings, it was to gaze on a spectacle, a heralded curiosity, amusing, melancholy, or scandalous, as the case might be. That noble political ideas did sometimes pass like dreams through the speculations of philosophers must be admitted, but it was only as literary aliment as with Glück and Piccini. It was only after the roar of the tempest of revolution had made itself heard, that all eyes fixed themselves earnestly and steadily on that point of the political firmament from which the deluge was seen sternly advancing, spreading terror and chaos everywhere, and scarcely reflecting the faintest rays of hope. From that time no nation has ceased to look upwards!

Everything belonging to the past, its wealth, its rank, its reputations, in short the whole fabric of society having crumbled, there arose universally a sentiment of equality that absorbed all minds. Every man said to his neighbor, "I am as good as you!" Law and authority once set aside, there remained only momentary individual rights; the casual conflict of these, similar to the contact of electric clouds, produced the passing explosion of the revolution. Here was an opportunity to reconstruct the social edifice! From this chaotic confusion, however, there issued, not social order but, on the contrary, a tempest of passion, which ended in terror. This reign of universal terror, like the rolling cylinder passing over the turf, simply prepared the bowed and prostrate heads of the people for despotism.

This despotism temporarily regenerating, was wholly of a new order. Based entirely on force, it revived nothing that could irritate the newborn spirit of equality. The names, the titles, the old fortunes, and the old reputations, formerly provocative of so much jealousy, remained entombed in the past;—all the new dignities and insignia that succeeded, far from being objects of envy, existed simply as stimulants to the aspirations of the new men. Along with old institutions, moreover, disappeared countless prejudices and the thousand absurd results of ancient ignorance. Thus disengaged from the ruins of a former period, the new spirit showed itself to be so superior to the old as already to demonstrate the benefit derived from the absence of former institutions. The despot knew how to profit by the light of a new epoch, and being himself a luminary, forestalled in his subordinates the false measures and narrow views of mediocrity, which, operating badly in the present, are always preparing still greater evils for posterity. Genius, when it strikes, strikes with the precision of lightning, whilst Ignorance descends broadcast, like the devastating hailstorm.

Let us now contemplate the effect of this tempest on the morals of the French.

Wide-spread terror and universal ruin, descending like a flood on the dissolute manners of the great and the rich, brought back into family life, and into a recognition of duty, the men whom prosperity had hitherto seduced therefrom. Virtue seemed now to have become the asylum of misery. It was, on the other hand, with horror, and as if to affright mankind, that the demons of the storm were observed to revel in all the exaggeration and nakedness of vice. But from so many dire misfortunes many unforeseen blessings were evoked.

Religion, the consoler of the unfortunate, deserted her insolent conquerors to minister to their victims, and the worship of the heart, not a prescribed ritual as in our days, succeeded to the immorality of the Revolution.

The old social barriers once removed, every avenue to fortune was opened to talent and courage; hence the prodigious impulse given to men of genius, the need of whom at this time, when all was to be recast, was deeply felt.* Hence the conquests of the French due to the superiority of their talents: hence the colossal grandeur of a man who could only perish through self-destruction.

After the paroxysm of the Revolutión had subsided in France, there prevailed universally a spirit of lassitude. In travelling over the South of France in 1810, I noticed that the dominant sentiment in every breast and in every place was a willingness to endure any of the evils of despotism rather than again encounter the risks of a second convulsion.† This lassitude continued to increase with the increase of the evil; all dazzling illusions subsided, and gave way to sad realities. And yet, although France was covered with ruins, one could scarcely believe that there lay still concealed beneath these ruins unheard of means of prosperity!

In these days, when all things are submitted to calculation, when planets and gases are

* Letters had become a place of refuge and repose at a time when, everybody and everything being suspected, there was no security anywhere else.

† This national disposition was afterwards misunderstood as well by those who wished to excite as by those who wished to prevent a second revolution.

weighed in a balance, the value of empires is also estimated with the like certainty.

The Revolution of 1789 was due to a deficit of fifty millions, a sum which the financial resources of that day could not provide for. The twenty-six years that followed cost the country in destruction of property, in extravagance, and in current expenses, at least four thousand million francs, perhaps double that sum;* and yet, strange to say, the same empire in 1824, apparently so exhausted, pressed forward, all but indifferent in bearing the burden of a debt of three thousand millions, besides reducing the interest of the public debt out of the general abundance. The wealth of a nation accordingly is not founded on its material basis, but rather on a moral basis; what process of calculation could ever have produced an estimate of the financial results which we of the present day admire in the now happy land of France!

This extraordinary financial phenomenon proves that national prosperity is to be measured according to the degree of activity that

* The assignats alone were said to amount in nominal value to the enormous sum of forty-five billions, according to Ramel, the successor of Cambon.

generally prevails, combined with the maintenance of order, that is to say, the existence of good laws. The Revolution produced national activity; the Emperor knew how to direct this spirit of activity with consummate ability. Under Buonaparte the French empire suffered under the enormous weight it was made to carry; but the giant was strongly constituted; all the talent and energy the nation possessed was brought into service, and a few years' repose sufficed to restore the nation to its pristine vigor.

Out of the revolutionary struggle exaggerated opinions were generated as a natural consequence. These opinions, repressed under Buonaparte, expanded prodigiously at his fall, and in doing so led to one of those reactions which are always so dangerous in politics.

It is the nature of every will to express itself by desires and in efforts as vigorous in degree as the repression is to which it is subjected. Let this repression be removed, and proportionally to the nature of the force that held it in check, so is its reaction; and as every action produces a reaction, it is evident that a prolonged reaction necessarily leads to oscillations, which, far from restoring tranquillity, renders its return still more remote.

Other dangers threaten the man who, instead of directing national excitement, would seek to check it. As we are only able to judge by our souvenirs, and incapable of estimating the future except by the past, it happens that men who are fondly attached to the past judge the present according to impressions derived from a former state of things; so that, far from attaining the desired end, they necessarily miss it in taking their stand-point at a non-existing period. These principles, well understood and generously applied by the authorities that have twice acted as restoratory agents in France, were not so acted upon subsequently by the party of the opposition. Hence new aggressions by the latter, who, considering themselves sustained by the nation, have continued to struggle against a power the strength of which they misconceived. Since the second struggle the authorities have abandoned the policy which these principles demanded; it remains to be seen whether they are not preparing further reactions against themselves in the future.

I may be permitted a few words on the exaggeration of religious ideas.

We discover an exaggeration of religious ideas in both the dominant faiths of Europe.

Among the Protestants, especially in Germany and in Switzerland, the reaction of religious ideas is due, much more due to theories of conscience than to ceremonial observances. In France, on the other hand, we find the religious polity everywhere strengthened; spiritual agents or soldiers are created and organized, and all places abound in missionaries, crosses, crucifixes, and images of suffering; the thunder of the preacher is everywhere heard producing unrestrained terror; the pulpits are transformed into volcanoes, where heaven and hell open out at will for the salvation or damnation of sinners. Among the Protestants of the North it is the conscience, it is religious revivals, which go on increasing without end, frequently resulting in insanity, as we see in Switzerland and Germany.*

* In Switzerland, near Berne, within a period of ten years, young girls have been known to smother their grandfathers; and lately, at Zurich, a young girl took the life of a sister, and then crucified herself, all with the very best of motives. Once admit that the religious revivals one experiences are the inspiration of God, and there is no limit to the faith attached to them, there is no limit to the vagaries of the imagination fed by religious excitement. Do not all men who believe themselves inspired pursue the same course, the prin-

There is, perhaps, at the present day, a spirit of emulation among Protestants which leads them to compete zealously with the Catholics; religious zeal is inconsiderately fomented by innumerable foolish pamphlets distributed with bibles, which, happening to accord with the present over-religious excitement of a few towns and villages, helps to swell to an unnatural degree, and beyond all reasonable limits, a very legitimate sentiment. To kindle too freely religious excitement, without sobering it down by the diffusion of knowledge, is productive of fanaticism, which is but the explosion of a feeling run mad. What will be the fate of nations when all these exaggerations and irrational notions come into conflict! If another Revolution is still dreaded, is it by fermenting fanaticism and exciting passion that its advent can be stayed?

A knowledge of the theory of reactions is most indispensable in the art of governing. It forms a branch of the theory of the sentiments, and is in itself a part of rational philosophy. The most brutal despotism recognises the moral

---

ciple being the same for all? Who dares doubt when Divinity speaks?

order of things, inasmuch as the Sultan, who severs heads at will, is first compelled to ascertain what pleases or displeases his janizaries and executioners.

The enemies of science firmly believe that an indifference to it will render them independent of its control. They are not aware that the subject about which they neglect to inform themselves is steadily sounding in our ears with the hum of many voices, and that it is shaping our destinies whether we hearken to its mandates or not. They are like the *bourgeois gentilhomme*, who was constantly indulging in good and bad prose without knowing it; they are unconsciously fashioning *something*, the only difference being this, that what they do not learn to do well, they are always learning to do badly. A patient who eats and drinks manufactures medicine for himself without knowing it, ignorant whether he is doing himself good or evil, surrendering himself to that principle which is always adverse to man's best interests—the capricious principle of chance.

Are not all human things under the dominion of thought? And is it not the thought which guides all our actions, and all our projects, that shapes the destiny of man? Let a man be ignorant of navigation, and he will be punished with shipwreck; let him be ignorant of commerce and ruin follows; let the art of living with our fellow-creatures be unknown to him, and he is punished for his ignorance. In all social actions, even in thought itself, man is a philosopher without being aware of it, that is to say, he acts according to some principle useful to the intelligent, destructive to the ignorant. In all our social actions we follow some vague theory of the moral sentiments; we desire to produce this or that effect on those around us, and that determines our will. Everybody has some particular theory of the human heart by which he regulates himself. Who is not aware that the most valuable of all knowledge is that which throws new light on man's knowledge of himself? Nobody desires to return evil for evil,—if this is done it is because man in his ignorance knows not how to act otherwise.

If there were a state of social harmony in which the happiness of all would be augmented by the happiness of each, ought we not fully to understand that state, without which there is no harmony on earth, and with which there is harmony for all? What knowledge, what study is equal to that of the human heart, the most neglected of all studies, and of all the most essential, particularly as it discloses the dangers of reactionary movements which, in retarding the great progress of the human mind, prepares unforeseen explosions, and which, in polluting the sources of intelligence, seems to place in question the destinies of humanity.

And let it not be said that it is not necessary to occupy oneself with rational philosophy, because it is not on a level with the physical sciences. All the sciences commenced by erring. Chemistry began with alchemy and astronomy with astrology. What was medicine a hundred years ago? What was the knowledge of man before the origin of the sciences? And what would we all be now without the labors of genius? What is there between civilization and barbarism, but the sciences, without which we would still be but the melancholy heirs of nomadic savages? If a knowledge of matter is of so much importance, that of the moral man is not less so. Does not the glory and welfare of nations depend upon it? How can men be successfully governed if their rulers do not properly understand them?

Ignorant of the interdependence of our sentiments we are like intoxicated men confined to a dark room,—we push, crowd, maul, and wound ourselves by a conflict of tastes and passions; whereas the study of the human heart would lead us to do only the evil which we would wish to do, and this evil, to the man of intelligence, would be much less than we imagine.

Sound rational philosophy is a science of the motive principles of man's nature; it is to human actions what mechanics is to the motion of bodies. Matter and mind are always and continually in the presence of man; they form the glory and the happiness of him who learns to subject them slowly to science and intelligence, as they form the torment of him who would through stupidity renounce reason without which there is no such thing as humanity.

* * * * *

Political theories present other phenomena than those of the religious world. A new element makes its appearance in connection with political theories, an element known to us under the name of liberal ideas, and which has thrown the whole system of politics into confusion.

By the Revolution a new impulse was given to thought; its demolitions prepared an open field for its development, added to which all eyes and interests centred upon public affairs. From the union of these three causes spring liberal ideas, that is to say the ideas of an enlightened era applied to the good of the state. It was not long before these ideas became hostile, and in this manner. The Revolution having shattered all thrones, and set aside the routine and customs of a former epoch, the kings reinstated in power, found their habits and customs in opposition to the new ideas called liberal. These new ideas were not vain chimeras; their results were seen to flourish in England; the friends of democratic ideas saw them take root in the United States of America; this prosperity of liberal ideas tended to excite emulation. There was no disposition on the part of enlightened men to copy these precise principles, but to apply them whenever they could be made useful; it being the province of mediocrity to copy, and of genius to employ, because it alone knows how to apply and to modify according to circumstances. There was a universal demand for constitutions, the most civilized nations regarding them as the first step towards liberty and a necessary result of civilization. The wisdom and generosity of the conquerors allowed them.

We have only to frequent the *salons*, and in the manners and customs of the men of all nations we discover that heads and their thoughts are no longer what they were. Social order is not the work of man; it is the natural product of the relationships which time and circumstance develop. From these relationships proceeds the birth equally of dependence and liberty. The servitude of the Turk who peaceably allows his head to be stricken off, is as natural as the Englishman's opposition to the slightest exercise of tyranny. The contrasts, which in one nation excite the astonishment of another, exist in every nation from epoch to epoch, from 1798 to 1824, as well as in all other epochs anterior to it.

The struggle, of a more or less animated character, which we contemplate in all nations of the present day, is but the natural movement of elements which are everywhere seeking to coalesce. The revolutionary tree of France, stripped of its branches at Waterloo, has not yet been fully articulated with the old royalty grafted upon its stock.

Internal policy and external relations are denaturalized by the war that is waged against liberal ideas, and all natural combinations have to yield to the fear which they engender. Instead of controlling men and events outside of itself, France destroys its natural friends to the great profit of its rivals; instead of making her distinguished men valuable to her she persecutes them to the great detriment of the public welfare. Does she not act like the man in the fable who exhausted himself in beating the image of a lion?

The natural relationships of nations, formerly constituting the basis of European policy, are no longer observed;. imaginary and factitious ones now replace them; battles now are fought with armies of opinions, and not with men; we see enemies cut to pieces like Milton's demons, to be set up again the first opportunity, and in improved shapes.

The real strength of a state consists of the fundamental relationships on which its power rests, and not of transient mutable opinions. For a state to oppose its tyranny to thought is to maintain a war against shadows. Opinions are the result of certain conditions of life and thought; they follow the reality as shadows follow instead of preceding bodies. It is as a reality—it is in its source—that we must combat it.

In vitium ducit culpæ fuga si caret arte.

Monarchies had unquestionably to guarantee themselves against the current, which could not be suddenly checked, of the terrible struggle that threatened to overthrow both people and kings: but the liberals, who are now hated and feared, do they not form the most enlightened class of the nation? With what is the great majority of these pretended enemies reproached, if not with an exaggeration of patriotic sentiment, which good kings share alike with them! The means of prosperity, of knowledge, of wealth, and, perhaps, of some germs of the higher virtues, are they not possessed by these men, who are only made enemies by the hatred shown them, and the persecutions they are made to endure?

The struggle we now witness is it not a combat between Spanish principles, the sad consequences of which we see developed in the South of France, and English principles, the glory of which at the North is spreading itself over every region of the Earth?

Instead of trampling upon, even educationally, the true germs of national virtue, instead of renouncing principles favorable to public prosperity, instead of treating as enemies the most distinguished men whose power can become so useful, would it not be better to employ these men with these principles than to reject as enemies that which constitutes the glory and prosperity of him who would know how to profit by it?

THE END.

CPSIA information can be obtained
at www.ICGtesting.com
Printed in the USA
LVHW100516130422
716029LV00002B/132

9 783752 595178